JOSÉ EDUARDO AGUALUSA

A Practical Guide to Levitation

STORIES

*Translated from the Portuguese
by Daniel Hahn*

archipelago books

First Archipelago Books Edition, 2023

"A Practical Guide to Levitation" was first published in *Words Without Borders* (2007),
"The Man with the Light" appeared in *Found in Translation*
(ed. Frank Wynne) in 2018, and "The Best Bed in the World" and
"The Outrageous Baobob" were published by Sublunary Editions (2019).

Library of Congress Cataloging-in-Publication Data available upon request.
ISBN 9781953861627

Archipelago Books
232 3rd Street #A111
Brooklyn, NY 11215
www.archipelagobooks.org

Distributed by Penguin Random House
www.penguinrandomhouse.com

Cover photo: Sebastião Salgado
Designed and typeset by Gopa & Ted2

This work is made possible by the New York State Council on the Arts
with the support of the Office of the Governor and the New York State
Legislature. Funding for the translation of this book was provided
by a grant from the Carl Lesnor Family Foundation.

This publication was made possible with support from the Nimick Forbesway Foundation, Lannan
Foundation, the National Endowment for the Arts, and The New York City Department of
Cultural Affairs. Funded by the DGLAB/Culture and the Camões Institute.

PRINTED IN CANADA

Contents

A Practical Guide to Levitation

Borges In Hell

JORGE LUÍS BORGES discovered he had died when, having closed his eyes the better to hear the distant murmur of the night as it grew over Geneva, he began to see. First he made out a red light, very intense, and understood that it was the blaze of the sun filtering through his eyelids. Then he opened his eyes, tilted his face to one side, and saw a row of dense green shadows. He was stretched out on his back in a plantation of banana trees. This put him in a bad mood. Banana trees?! He had always imagined paradise as a kind of library: an unending succession of corridors, staircases, and more corridors, leading to more staircases and further corridors, and all of them piled up to the ceiling with books.

Borges got to his feet. He straightened himself up with some difficulty, uncomfortable within his own suddenly rejuvenated body (when we die we are reincarnated young and Borges no longer remembered what that was like). He walked slowly between the banana trees. It was quite unlikely, he thought, that he would run into somebody he knew here, that is to say, somebody by whom he had read anything. Or somebody *about* whom he had read anything. In which latter case they would be just a little less known, or a little less somebody, or both.

The plantation stretched out for all eternity. He began to be tormented by a suspicion: perhaps, after all, he was not in paradise, but in hell. Wherever he looked he could see only the wide green leaves, the heavy yellow bunches and above this unchanging landscape a vastly blue sky. Borges really was so sorry about the lack of books. If only there had at least been some tigers – metaphorical tigers, obviously, with a secret alphabet engraved in their dorsal markings – if there'd been a labyrinth someplace, or a pink corner (a corner would be enough for him), but no: all he could make out were banana trees, banana trees, more banana trees. Banana trees as far as the eye could see.

Untiring, though with growing tedium, he made his way through the infinite plantation. It was like he was walking in circles. It was like he wasn't walking at all. He missed his blindness. When he was blind, what he couldn't see had had more color than this – and then there was also the mystery, of course. How is it possible for a man to die in Switzerland and be resuscitated for life eternal amid banana trees?

Borges didn't like Latin America. Argentina, as is well known, is a European country (or almost), which to its great misfortune just happens to border Brazil, Chile, Uruguay, and Paraguay. To Borges that had almost always been a thorn buried deep in his soul. That and his neighborhood. The Indians he could handle, actually. They had supplied good motifs for literature, and besides, they were dead. The worst were the blacks and the mestizos, people who were able to transform the great drama of life – of life, my God! – into a noisy party. Borges felt European. He liked to read the Greek classics (he would have liked to have read them in Greek). He liked the potent silence of old cathedrals.

That was when he saw her. Ahead of him, a woman was floating, pale and naked, over the banana trees. The woman was asleep, with her face turned toward the sun and her hands resting on her breast, and she was so very beautiful, but to Borges this didn't matter all that much (his specialty had always been tigers). Horrified, he understood the mistake. God had confused him with another Latin American writer. This paradise had been constructed, could only have been constructed, with Gabriel García Márquez in mind.

Jorge Luís Borges sat down on the damp earth. He raised an arm, picked a banana, peeled it, and ate it. He thought about Gabriel García Márquez and once again felt the unbearable torment of envy. One day the Colombian writer would close his eyes the better to hear the distant murmur of the night, and when he re-opened them he would be lying on his back on the cold flagstones of a library. He would walk down the corridors, he would climb the stairs, then up more corridors, even more stairs and further corridors, and in each one he would find books, millions of books. An infinite labyrinth, lined to the ceiling with shelves, and on those shelves every book written or yet to be written, every possible combination of words in all the languages of mankind.

Jorge Luís Borges peeled another banana and at that moment a smile – or something like a smile – lit up his face. He was beginning to make out, in this cruel error, an unexpected meaning: it being the case that the other man's paradise was now his hell, then his own paradise would, surely, have to be a hell to the other man.

Borges finished peeling his banana and ate it. It was good. What a good hell this was.

How Sweet It Is to Die in the Sea

For Mia Couto, he knows why

V IRGÍNIA SEEMED a vaguely anachronistic name to me, almost ridiculous – until I met her. It was the day I turned fifty. By then I had already lost the brilliant future that, in the recent past, some critics had promised me. Those same critics hadn't liked my latest novel. They mocked it, they destroyed it. After that I never managed to finish so much as another short story. I'd write half a dozen pages and then stop for lack of ideas and conviction. Conviction, incidentally, is much more important than a good idea. I would rub everything out. Then I would start again, then I'd remember the reviews, and I'd rub it all out again. It was bad. Real bad. I went back to drinking. At night I would lie down in bed, but I didn't fall asleep. I got up and drank. Manuela, my first wife, asked for a divorce. She said:

"I hate losers. Most of all I hate losers who drink too much."

I didn't argue with her. I didn't have the heart to argue. I packed my bags and moved to a small apartment, on the other side of the road, to stay close to the kids. After three months, however, I realized I couldn't pay the rent for much longer. I swallowed my pride and asked for asylum at my mom's. I went back to writing reviews for newspapers and literary magazines. I used a number of pseudonyms, first because I didn't want my detractors to rejoice at my no longer being able to live off my copyrights alone; and also because I could thereby, without any risk, trash my fellow writers, including some friends, or rather, ex-friends, people who'd distanced themselves from me, out of fear, presumably, that my failure might infect them. For the record: writers on the way up do not like to be seen with writers on the way down.

I took particular pleasure in destroying the debut novel by a young talent who, before he had dared to take that step, had become relatively well known as a literary critic. Américo, I'll call him, had been the first to throw stones at me. The guy was nearly two meters tall, very blond and very white, of an absent-minded kind of beauty, like an angel on vacation. I used the exact same technique with which he'd destroyed my book, including some of his own killer phrases, to clip his wings. My only happy moments in those days were the ones I spent at the computer writing that review, and then reading them in the newspaper and hearing the comments, the laughter, from other critics and writers.

That was my life, then, or what was left of it, when I got an invitation to take part in a series of panel discussions (at the festival in Paraty) on the future of the Portuguese-language novel. In Brazil, unlike Portugal, my books had always been very positively received by critics. Regrettably, they've sold little. The gathering went well. I did my thing. I told worn-out jokes as though I'd just invented them myself that very moment. I illustrated fanciful opinions with true stories. I laughed, I was moved. At the end, the audience rose to their feet to applaud me. I still had three days before I was due to return to Lisbon. My talk was in the morning. There were another two that afternoon. I decided to give them a miss. I put on a bathing suit, thinking, as I put it on, how archaic and formal that word sounded in contrast to the Brazilian word *sunga*. "In my day, we used to go to the baths at Estoril," I heard my maternal grandfather's (weary) voice. In that local word *sunga* you can sense the echo of drums. My grandfather really did use bathing suits. He would go to the baths like other gentlemen would go to mass. He would never have worn a thing called a *sunga*. I slipped a pair of Havaianas onto my feet and went down to the front desk. The receptionist, a girl with deep eyes and cascading hair, laughed for no reason when I asked her for a towel. She handed me the towel and laughed again. She explained I just needed to go straight up the road, past the little stone bridge, to get to one of the loveliest beaches in the city. I walked about twenty

9

minutes till I found it. A perfect bay, ringed from behind by tall mountains of a ravishing green, and in front of it the calm sea and the flocks of islands. Beside the sand, in the shadow of some trees that were low but thick with foliage, there were three or four round tables, and half a dozen plastic chairs, light in color, punished by the sun: a bar. I sat down and ordered a caipirinha. I thought about my imminent return to Lisbon and a heavy sadness closed around me like a fist. I was turning fifty but nobody, not even my mother, had called to wish me a happy birthday. I was taken by a stupid desire to cry. The owner of the little bar, a sleepy, extinguished mulatto – extinguished truly in the sense of a candle whose flame has gone out – dressed only in an old pair of blue shorts, brought me the caipirinha and then moved away, humming quietly. I recognized the tune before grasping, as if in a revelation, the meaning of the words:

> *How sweet to die at sea,*
> *amid the sea's green waves.*
> *So to the sea's green waves,*
> *to drown himself he fled.*
> *And there he found a place*
> *in the green waves of the sea,*
> *And made his wedding bed*
> *in Yemanjá's embrace.*

I can't swim. I grew up in a land of fishermen, the son and grandson of fishermen on my father's side, but I never learned to swim. My father couldn't swim either. My paternal grandfather drowned when the small boat he was on capsized as it was coming into the harbor. The boat was called *Flower of the Atlantic*.

There was nobody on the beach. I got up and walked down into the sea. The water was so light, I could barely feel it on my body. The ground didn't feel like it was made of sand but of some substance that was soft and warm, which had taken a liking to my feet. I no longer felt sad, on the contrary, there was a kind of euphoria now pushing me forward. I would not go back to Lisbon. When, the following day, the newspapers reported my death, perhaps then Manuela would feel sorry for the way she had treated me. The same critics who had condemned me would line up to exalt my work, and I would return, albeit dead, to the bestseller lists. Américo would try to hide his crime but he would be exposed, and no newspaper would ever accept his reviews again. I was getting so enthusiastic that I had to hold myself back from running. Dying, yes, but slowly. I walked a hundred meters or so, a hundred and fifty, the water always at my knees. I walked another hundred. The island, in the distance, got a little closer. I kept walking. I could already make out a few of the details of the island: a ruined jetty, part of a wall glittering in the sun; yet still the water had not even come to my waist. I realized, when I looked back, that I had walked a long way. The coastline was as far away as the island. You could get to Angola on foot at this rate. I lost heart. It was like trying to drown myself in a soup bowl. I lay on my back and shut my eyes. My hands touched the muddy bottom. I remained like that for some time. The sun prickled my face. I dreamed of algae, jellyfish, shipwrecked caravels, mermaids drowned in the shallow tide.

"You're a writer?"

I opened my eyes and there she was, standing between me and the green islands, as if she had been cut out of a tourist postcard. She was wearing an elusive burnt-yellow bikini, which made her seem even darker and, in a strange way that I can't quite explain, almost fierce.

"My name's Virgínia . . ."

The receptionist. Virgínia, aged eighteen, only child of Dona Marta, the hotel's owner. She put her long arms around my neck and kissed me on the lips. I didn't go back to Lisbon. I married Virgínia three months later and, at the invitation of Dona Marta, who had always liked me, I started to manage the hotel.

Does it irritate you (I'm addressing the critics here) that I should summarize my love story in one brief paragraph, along with the fine friendship I established with Dona Marta? You think it's too abrupt? I'm sorry about that, but it really was very fast. Virgínia put her long arms around me, held the nape of my neck in both hands, kissed me, and the next moment I was married.

Five years went by (also very quickly). Dona Marta died from a mugger's bullet, in a suburb of Rome, the city where her family had come from, and where she'd moved for fear of the violence in Brazil. And then, one rainy July afternoon, I saw a very tall young man walk into the hotel, his clothes drenched, sticking to his body, and his very blond hair dripping with water. He stood in front of me like an amazed cherub:

"Pacheco?!" There was a kind of shock in his voice. "Pacheco, the writer?"

I recognized him by his height. It was harder to recognize myself in his incredulity, so long had it been since I'd heard my real name. I hadn't been Pacheco, the writer, for quite a while. I was Mr. Pedro now, the Portuguese man who'd married Virgínia, Dona Marta's son-in-law, the owner of the Perfect Loves Hotel. In short: a good guy, not exactly young any more, balding, but still attractive, nice-looking. The young man insisted:

"I'm sorry, aren't you Pacheco, the writer Pedro Pacheco?"

"Américo?"

The past came back to me like a body-blow. I felt an ancient bitterness rising into my soul. I hesitated a moment between hugging him and smacking him. I hugged him:

"What are you doing here?"

Américo had arrived in Paraty that same afternoon to take part in a series of panel discussions on the state of the Portuguese-language novel. "A lot of people have come from Lisbon," he said, and he cited various familiar names. I asked him (because I felt I needed to ask him something) how many novels he'd published now. Américo looked at me with ill-disguised suspicion:

"How many? Just one, *Of Love and Death* – you didn't read it?"

"No, no!" I realized that my double denial, an excess of vehemence, might seem stranger still, and I attempted to correct it: "No, no, my friend, unfortunately I haven't read it. I've been living here, in Paraty, for almost five years. Hardly any news from Portugal reaches me here."

Américo leaned forward slightly, fixed his lucid angel-eyes on me. He wanted, perhaps, to confirm that I had not, in fact, come to read the vile things he had written about my last book; either that or he knew the true identity of the person who had destroyed his first, his only novel.

"Have you heard of a guy called Camilo Durão?"

I denied it, horrified: "Camilo what?" Camilo Durão was the pseudonym I had used to murder *Of Love and Death*. I didn't regret it. As best I could remember, the novel really was mediocre, boring, a little over two hundred pages that were sweating from the effort of seeming original. Américo was part of that group of writers quite capable of affirming, with tears in their eyes, their total dedication to literature – "if I don't write, I waste away," or "oh, writing for me is like breathing" – despite the fact, unfortunately, that they have nothing to say. Having conquered the final page, I don't think there'd be many readers who could summarize the plot. I'm not sure it even had a plot. Still, Américo pretended to believe me. He clapped me on the back with the manly delight of somebody who has run into an old drinking buddy from his wild youth, and gave me a big, magnanimous smile:

"What about you? Have you written much?"

I hate him. I hate it when people slap me on the back. Besides, he *knew* I had never been able to write again. I didn't tell him this, of course, I changed the subject, and amid laughter and recollections I showed him the hotel. Finally I invited him to stay in the best room. That night I had dinner with him and the other Portuguese writers in a small restaurant overlooking the river. Virgínia liked Américo at once.

It has only been three months since that night, no longer than a sigh, but to me it feels like it all happened in a different incarnation. The German (I must tell you about him) was also there. Even now, after everything that's happened, I can't help thinking of Martin with affection, I can't help missing him. I met him not long after arriving in Paraty. Here, where he lived for more than fifteen years, everybody called him The German, but Martin Ries was a Luxembourger. His small travel agency, *Man at Sea*, organized diving excursions for the tourists. The German was a tall, solid man with copper-colored hair cropped short and an explosive temper which led him to perpetrate some crazy things only to, later – the very next moment – come to his senses and transform into the sweetest person in the world. We played tennis on Tuesdays and Thursdays. On Saturdays we played chess.

Américo stayed in Paraty for a couple of weeks then returned to Portugal. Before leaving, he insisted on interviewing me for a literary magazine of which he himself was the editor. He sent me the magazine a few days later. I thought the way he presented me really rather nice. Too nice, perhaps. I was left with the suspicion that he was trying to excuse himself for the way he had destroyed my novel. The second week in October, I received an invitation to São Luís, up in Maranhão, to a festival of Portuguese-language cinema, where a film based on one of my novels was in competition. I said goodbye to Virgínia and set off for Rio by bus, planning to fly from there to São Luís, making the most of the stop to call in at my publishers, to buy some books, and settle two or three little bureaucratic problems. When I arrived in Rio, however, I learned that the film had been withdrawn from the festival, due to some dispute or other with the producer, and I gave up on the trip. I called Virgínia to tell her I was intending to come back home that night; the exact moment she answered, however, an idea (a stupid one) occurred to me: I should surprise her.

"Honey?! It's me. Yes, I'm already in São Luís . . ."

I told her I'd be staying a week in Maranhão as planned, that it was very sunny, that my chest was already aching from missing her so much, etc., those kinds of things, and I hung up.

I rented a car and that same night, after a quiet dinner with my publisher, I returned to Paraty. By the time I arrived at the hotel, I was exhausted, and dawn was breaking. I went inside, carrying the small yellow suitcase I always travel with, a bag of groceries, and a huge bunch of flowers, I found no one at reception (perhaps Adriano, who does the night shift, had gone to the bathroom), and climbed the solid wooden staircase to the second floor, where our apartment was, trying to move as silently as I could. I put down the suitcase, and the bag, but not the bunch of flowers, and opened the door. Virgínia was stretched out on her front, on the bed, totally naked. Her beauty, so exposed in this way, open and defenseless, in the harsh morning light, dazzled me. Only then did I see the man. He looked up, startled, the moment I dropped the flowers:

"Pacheco?! But . . . what the fuck are you doing here?"

It was his tone that annoyed me most, so surprised and yet

17

commanding, very confident, and that faintly affected accent, which a certain class of Portuguese, the same people who frequent the fashionable bars and gossip magazines, like to cultivate. Américo got up and I noticed three things:

1. That he was wearing black socks.
2. That he had his gleaming blond hair impeccably combed back.
3. That he was shorter than me, thinner, and without the slightest doubt, much less well favored for the games of love (I imagine there will be critics who'll want to mock this expression; fine by me, whatever, choose another. Honestly, I don't give a crap about you critics).

Virgínia was a heavy sleeper. She hadn't woken. I said nothing. I took three steps toward Américo, gave him a valiant kick in the shins, which isn't the most honest of blows, I realize, but it always works, and when he leaned forward in a spasm of pain, I broke his nose with a single punch. I left, slamming the door, bounded down the stairs, and a moment later I was on the street. As I ran I thought about how I should go back and talk to Virgínia, I thought about the shame that would come the following day, when the whole city learned of the affair, I thought about how I had nothing left now, not even that shame, I thought about how I should have punched

Américo a second time, I thought about this with some joy, and I thought with horror about what I was going to do next. Suddenly I found myself outside The German's house. I hesitated a moment, then knocked on the door. When he opened it, I fell sobbing into his arms. I struggled to make myself understood. Martin looked at me bewildered:

"You caught Virgínia with another guy?! No, no! Virgínia would never do that. It's not possible . . ."

I saw him change. It was as if he were the injured party. He pulled on his pants and a T-shirt while simultaneously slapping and kicking the furniture and the walls.

"What a total slut! Women are all the same!"

I snapped out of it, and tried to calm him:

"Hey, man, Martin, maybe she's got some kind of explanation . . ."

The German threw me a twisted look as he opened a drawer and took out a pistol. I don't know anything about firearms. It was a small, metallic implement, it looked like a toy. If some kid had tried to hold me up on the street with a weapon like that, I would have laughed in his face. I saw Martin put it in his pants pocket. He roared:

"An explanation?! The whore was there, in bed, with another guy, and you think she has an explanation? Just don't leave this house, fuck's sake, wait here till I get back!"

He opened the door and disappeared. I went to the kitchen, took a beer out of the fridge, and sat down to drink. I was still there when one of the neighbors burst in:

"Pacheco?! What the fuck are you doing here?! Come quick. The German's shot your wife . . ."

He killed her. Two bullets in the chest. Then he forced Américo to kneel down (that's what the police investigators suppose) and shot him in the back of the neck. Finally he put the weapon in his own mouth and fired. Four bullets, three dead. A drama that for weeks on end puzzled the city.

"Why?!"

I know why. I knew it the moment I saw Martin leaving the house, shouting, to kill Virgínia and her lover. I confirmed it, some days later, when, tidying my late wife's papers, I found a letter signed by Martin, in which he addressed Virgínia as "my little chocolate bonbon." It seemed so very sordid, I thought. The intrigue I can accept. Even the double betrayal. What annoys me, and what I cannot forgive, neither Virgínia nor Martin, is the style. For the love of God: little chocolate bonbon! There were three other letters written in an ignoble Portuguese, and in each one Martin referred to Virgínia as bonbon. Or worse: baby squirrel, little vixen, bunny rabbit.

I don't remember much of the first few days after the tragedy. I spent them drinking. Bit by bit, however, I began to calm down. One afternoon, as I was walking along the beach, I realized that Martin had, with those four shots, solved all my problems, including those I didn't even know I had. Let's take a look:

1. He killed my critic.
2. He killed my wife's two lovers.
3. He killed my wife.
4. He secured me a rich inheritance.
5. He supplied me with a good plot for a novel.

I started writing again. I write with urgency. If I don't write, I don't die, I don't waste away, and I don't even risk going hungry. I've got my little hotel. I lead a peaceful life. The best thing about old age is that we no longer need to prove ourselves. I like walking on the beach in the early evening. I step into the tranquility of the waters and lie on my back, floating. I love it.

A Practical Guide to Levitation

I DON'T LIKE PARTIES. The idle chat, the smoke, the fatuous talk of drunks. I find them all tiresome. Plastic plates annoy me even more. And plastic cutlery. And plastic cups. I'm served roasted rabbit on a plastic plate, forced to eat it with plastic cutlery, on my lap because there's no more room at the table. Inevitably the knife breaks. The meat is thrown onto my trousers. I spill my wine. Besides which, I can't stand rabbit. I make a great effort not to be noticed, but there's always some woman who at a given moment pulls at my arms – "let's dance!" – and off I go, crawling along behind her, stunned by the shrill dissonance of the perfume and the volume of the music. At the end of the number – somewhat humiliated because, I confess, I've got two left feet – I pour myself a whisky, with a lot of ice, someone shakes me – what's up, pal, something annoy you? and I, forcing a smile, forcing myself to burst out laughing, like the rest of the crowd – what, me? annoyed? What could have annoyed me? the need to be jolly calls to me, and I shout back,

23

"I'm coming, I'm coming," and return to the dance floor, and pretend to be dancing, pretend to be happy, leaping to the right, leaping to the left, until they've forgotten I'm there.

That night I was almost at that point of being forgotten when I noticed a tall figure, dressed all in white, like a lily, white hair flowing loose over his shoulders, with a serious expression, circling the cod pasties. The man seemed to be there by mistake. At once I thought this man must be as abandoned as I was. He could have been me, but for the clothes, as I never wear white. White doesn't really suit my line of work. Bright colors still less. I follow tradition, and dress in black. I approached the man, with the solidarity of a fellow castaway, and held out my hand.

"I'm Whoever," I said to him, "I sell coffins."

The man's hand was limp and pale in mine. There was a vague, dark shine to his eyes, like a moonlit lake. Most people are unable to hide their shock, or their laughter, depending on the circumstances, when they hear the word "coffins." Some of them hesitate. You sell coffee? No, I correct them, coffins. This man, however, was unperturbed.

"There's no such thing as a real name," he replied, with a thick Pernambuco accent. "But you can call me Emmanuel Subtle."

This was in Rio de Janeiro, in Jardim Botânico. His accent was as dislocated as mine, maybe even more so. Almost ridiculous.

"And what do you do?"

"I teach . . ."

"Ah, really? What do you teach?"

Emmanuel Subtle shook back his hair distractedly.

"Levitation."

"Levitation?!"

"You know – *levitation* – a psychic, animist, spiritualist phenomenon where someone or something is raised from the ground for
no apparent cause but merely through the power of the mind. The
mind mobilizes ectoplasmic fluids that are capable of overpowering
gravity. I teach levitation techniques. Without wires or any other
base tricks."

"Interesting! Interesting!" I replied, buying myself time to think.
"And do you have many students?"

The man gave me a serious smile; no, he didn't. Not a lot of people are interested in levitating nowadays. These are sad times. The
triumph of materialism has corrupted everything. There really isn't
much vocation for spiritual work anymore. Not much vocation, nor
much mind-power, I suggested timidly. Right, Emmanuel Subtle
agreed, shaking back his white hair again, nor much mind-power.
People prefer to keep their feet firmly planted on the ground. And
did he himself levitate? I wanted to know. That is, did he practice
this forgotten art often? Emmanuel Subtle smiled, engrossed:

"Not a day goes by that I don't. Levitation, my dear sir, is the most complete of exercises. Five minutes suspended, first thing in the morning, at the crack of dawn, will stimulate all your vital organs and revive your soul."

Sometimes he even found himself levitating by accident. He told me how Saint José of Cobertino – who lived from 1603 to 1663 – used to suffer sudden attacks of weightlessness whenever something moved him. Terrified, he would call these episodes "my dizzy spells." One Sunday during Mass he was abruptly elevated into the void and for several long minutes hovered anxiously over the altar, amid the sharp candle flames and the howls of the devout, and was severely burned. The church made him stay away from all public rites for thirty-five years as a result of these extravagant tendencies, but even this didn't prevent his fame from spreading. One evening, as the holy man wandered the monastery gardens in the company of a Benedictine monk, a gust of wind dragged him suddenly up to the topmost branches of an olive tree. Unfortunately, he – like cats and balloons – turned out to have a great propensity for getting up there, and none at all for getting back down, and he had to be rescued by the monks with the help of a stepladder. I murmured something about the mystical calling of olive trees and the tendencies they've demonstrated over centuries for attracting demiurges and saints. Emmanuel Subtle ignored my observation. The Saint

José of Cobertino case, he explained, served to illustrate the dangers involved in a lay person – even one supremely talented – practicing the art of levitation without the presence of a master.

"Would you put a Ferrari in the hands of a child? Of course not!"

I agreed at once. And, God, naturally I wouldn't trust myself with one either!

"Levitation is not for just anyone," Emmanuel Subtle continued, over-enunciating each word. "Levitation requires faith, perseverance, and something else besides: responsibility. Would you like to try?"

And then he set out his terms. Four hundred *reais* a month. Four times a week, an hour and a half per session. Naturally, he added, there was no chance of seeing any results before the third or fourth month.

"And if there are no results at all?"

Emmanuel Subtle reassured me. In three months, properly guided, even an elephant could levitate. And even if I proved myself as bad a levitator as I was a dancer (only then did I realize he had spent the entire evening observing me), he would give me a push himself. He cited the story of the famous English medium, Daniel Douglas Home, who in the thirties challenged the traditional British sangfroid by making pianos and other heavy objects float. One evening – so the story goes – he brought an ox into the ballroom of a rich industrialist, and lifted it up clean into the air. There the ox was, right up there with the chandeliers – high up and brightly lit – when for some reason, through some distraction or a temporary fading of his faith, he (the medium) lost his strength, the channels of ectoplasmic fluid broke, and the animal hurtled down with a brutal din, down onto two of his attendants.

"Did they die?"

"What do you think?" He sighed. "Aeronautical history is full of tragedies, some small, some great. But that doesn't stop us taking airplanes."

I turned down his invitation. The party was coming to an end. An old black man, who had once been very famous as a footballer, was dancing alone, tears in his eyes, set apart from the music – we'll call it music, a mixture of car alarms – hoarse and weary – and wrenching metal. Two very blonde, very languid girls were on a sofa sleeping in each other's arms. I knew no one. No one knew me.

"But I wonder whether perhaps you know anyone who offers invisibility classes? Now that's something I would be interested in."

Emmanuel Subtle looked at me with disdain. He didn't reply. And from the entrance hall, as I chose a suitably discreet umbrella – to go with my line of work – from a wet mass of them, I could see the Brazilian making his way through the thick smoke and collapsing onto the sofa, beside the two blonde girls. I saw him close his eyes. He crossed his arms over his thin chest. He seemed to be smiling. I've met some rather odd people at these parties. You can find anything here. The strangest occupations. I know, of course, that this just depends on your point of view. I, for example, sell coffins. My father sold coffins. My grandfather sold coffins. I grew up with it. To me it seems even prosaic. I know I would prefer to give levitation classes. But too bad. I can console myself with the knowledge that death is the best trade to be in. As my grandfather used to say, there's only one thing that worries me: immortality.

The Robbery

JULIANA STOPPED her car at the red light. What was she thinking about at that exact moment? In the days that followed, this
was the one thing that would trouble her. She insists that she had
just discovered something very important. But since she was half-
asleep – after twelve hours' working in the hospital E.R. – the like-
lihood is that it wasn't important in the least.

(I once had a dream that a cat, big as an ox, whispered a line
of poetry to me. In my dream it was the most extraordinary line.
Nothing I had written up until that point, since I was twenty, was
worth as much as that line. I struggled to wake up. I believed that
I was getting up, several times, only to discover immediately that I
was still plunged in the deep waters of sleep. Finally, I managed to
open my eyes, sat up in bed, found a pencil on the bedside table
and scribbled down the line on the cover of a book – Langston
Hughes's *The Big Sea*. I woke the next morning with a bitter taste
in my mouth and the troubling feeling that something astonishing

had happened. I remembered the dream, the cat grazing in an enormously green meadow, but not the line. Just as well, I thought, that I'd written it down. I grabbed hold of the book and read: "The day was so full of onions.")

Let us return to that moment when Juliana, gripping the steering wheel with desperate strength, so that the current of sleep would not drag her off, stopped her car at the red light. She was thinking, perhaps, about onions. Or not: we might accept the fact that, as she insists, she had just discovered something transcendent. We will never know. The right-hand door opened and a boy of about fifteen, with the volatile body of a classical ballerina, got into the car. By the time Juliana realized what was going on, there were another two young guys in the backseat.

The early hours of the morning were stretching over the city. The herons were still sleeping, so very elegant, in the branches of the casuarina trees. The waters of the lagoon were shining lethargically. Jesus Christ was floating, on his back, lit up by the melancholy glow of the floodlights. Juliana realized she could not count on him. The kid, the one next to her, showed her a revolver:

"So here's the thing, honey, either you hand over your purse or you take a bullet."

Juliana rested her face on the steering wheel. She'd seen a lot over the last twelve hours: girls yanked from the fierce ineptitude of favela abortionists, an old woman who'd been raped, men cut with knives, a youth with two bullets lodged in his spine following a pointless fight at a bar. He'd live. He'd live forever in a wheelchair.

"Hey, bruh," whispered one of the boys. "Looks like she's fallen asleep."

"Oh man, come on!" the other was stunned. "Where's her respect! When have you ever seen somebody fall asleep during a robbery?"

Sleeping would be really nice. Juliana turned toward him:

"You want to know something? I'm a doctor, I'm not scared of dying. It's only being crippled that scares me. I'm going to take hold of that gun now and point it at my heart. Then you can shoot."

She unbuttoned her blouse, took the kid's hand, shocked at her own firmness, and pressed the revolver to her chest.

"Kill me!"

The boy looked at her, frightened:

"No way I'm killing anyone, lady, what are you saying?"

"You won't kill me? Get out of my car, then! . . ."

"Let's get out of here, bruh," one of the two kids begged, "this woman's nuts."

The three of them got out. Juliana was left alone. What was it she'd been thinking about before she was interrupted? In the days that followed, this was the one thing that would trouble her.

If Nothing Else Works, Read Clarice

I'M AFRAID of turning on the TV, like getting onto the subway at rush hour, and having somebody carelessly or maliciously treading on my intelligence: "I'm sorry, OK?! I didn't mean it!" I'll turn on the set, hunched in my corner, pretending I'm not even there, but if by chance my eyes happen to stumble upon some barbaric-looking guy, I'm out of there. Then I shut my eyes and dream up a fish. It was an old Pernambuco fisherman who taught me that. I was sitting on the sands of Itamaracá, with a pad of paper on my lap, finishing a watercolor. He came up behind me and watched for a moment:

"Why are you doing that?" he asked. "You're never going to fit the sea in there!"

He sat beside me. He told me that sometimes, when he woke up, his humanity would ache, there on the left side of his chest. Then he would walk down to the beach, stretch out on his back on the sand, and dream up a fish.

"It was Clarice, you know? She's the one who initiated me."

At the time, I didn't understand who the old man was referring to. He started out dreaming up small, very rudimentary fish, just a quick flash of silver, just a light comma glittering in the air, but with time, as his technique developed, he started to dream up groupers, itajaras, even swordfish. His ambition was to dream up a whale. A blue whale.

"Keep alert to the color of the waters," he warned me. "For example, in the morning, really nice and early, if the water's smooth and silvery, it's a good time to dream up shad. The Atlantic tarpon, which is one of our fish, a big thing, is often dreamed up after it rains, when the rivers nighten the sea. Whereas a jack, well, a jack is better to dream up when the sea goes blue."

"And mermaids?"

He looked at me, amazed:

"Mermaids? What use are mermaids? Mermaids are badly dreamed creatures, like platypuses or generals. You'll have to do better than that."

I've been trying. I never learned the fisherman's name. He was a tall fellow, upright as a post, with blazing eyes and healthy skin stretched over his bones. He had a voice so clear and warm that, at night, as he spoke, it was as if he were spitting fireflies. A voice like that you should be able to leave somebody in a will. It reminded me of Fernando Alves's. They said on the island that the old man had spent three weeks lost at sea. He was saved by a miracle, because on the thirteenth day Our Lady of Aparecida appeared to him on his sloop, bearing a leg of pork and a liter bottle of Coca-Cola. He denied this miracle to me himself, actually a bit irritated:

"Our Lady of Aparecida? What are you talking about, 'Our Lady,' kid?! It was Clarice Lispector! . . ."

Every fisherman's tale has its exaggerations, sometimes even barefaced lies, or it wouldn't be a fisherman's tale. On this point, however, I am peremptory (I'm using that word for the first time in my life; can't you see how it shines?) – he read! He was a great admirer of Clarice Lispector and Alberto Caeiro. He told me that Clarice had appeared to him in the early hours of the morning bearing a copy of *The Apple in the Dark*, and read the entire novel to him. Then, when she thought he was more himself again, she taught him how to dream up fish.

"Dreaming up fish is good for the soul. Remember that for every bad man in the world there are a thousand good fish in the sea."

My fisherman didn't have a television set. Sometimes he happened to linger at a bar, or on the square (there was a TV on the square), and the roar of other people's wars would steal his sleep. Other people's mistakes made him suffer. He would walk around the island with *The Hour of the Star* under his arm, trying, without success, to convert other people. I was the only one to pay him any attention.

"If nothing else works, read Clarice."

One afternoon I saw him dream up a dolphin.

"That was my first mammal," he said to me afterward, exhausted at the effort. "I'm going to try for a killer whale next week."

I never went back to Itamaracá, I never saw him again, but by my reckoning he should have managed to dream up his blue whale by now. He would have launched it into the sea, a hundred and thirty tons of pure dream, and its song would now be echoing through the waters. One day the whales will come to save mankind.

Catalog of Shadows

For Kelly Cristina

A T FIRST, I laughed about what had happened. An unamused
sort of laugh, the way unfortunate souls laugh when they find
themselves caught in ridiculous situations by TV cameras. It felt
like one of those literary games so beloved by Jorge Luís Borges,
a tired old trick with mirrors, with impossible objects and ancient
books appearing out of nowhere to unsettle reality. It was Pedro
Rosa Mendes who discovered the book at an old dealer's in Alcân-
tara, in the state of Maranhão, hidden between volumes of nineteen-
forties Brazilian poetry. My friends know that I have, for many long
years, been nurturing a small monstrous library. I include in it all
manner of errors, aberrations and atrocities, but also miracles and
wonders, from works with foolish or disgusting titles to unabashed
plagiarisms, volumes with upside-down covers, others with serious
spelling mistakes in the actual title, difficult utopias that no one

would ever read. I have kept, for example, the work of an obscure Angolan writer, Marcial Faustino, which comprises only a dedication and three short poems. A note on the back declares confidently that it is a novel. The thickness of the volume, a hundred and eighty-seven pages of it, is made up by the dedication, surely the longest in universal literature. The author begins by dedicating the book to "our much-missed President Agostinho Neto," for about twenty-five pages, explaining the reason for his devotion, and then to his wife, thirty-something pages, to each of his twenty-two children, and so on it goes. Exceptionally interesting, that dedication. I can only presume it is – and in that, I can see a brilliant piece of literary daring – a novel disguised as a dedication.

"Do you know this one?"

I took the book from my friend's hand: *Catalog of Shadows*, by Alberto Caeiro, Ibis Publishing. A note on the final page indicated that any correspondence for the author or publisher should be directed to no.15 Calçada de Eleguá, São Paulo, Brazil. I leafed through it quickly and didn't recognize a single line. The style, however, stunned me – unmistakably Pessoa. That was when I remembered Borges.

"Maybe it's simply" – ventured my friend, stroking his chin – "an obscure Brazilian who happens to be the namesake of the more famous Portuguese heteronym."

It couldn't be that simple. The coincidence of names was not what really troubled me, it was the coincidence of genius. I put the book away between *As Quibíricas*, by Frey Ioannes Garabatus, aka António Quadros, and a rare edition of *Luuanda*, by Luandino Vieira, which an agent of the P.I.D.E. secret police had printed in Lisbon in 1965. António Quadros, the Portuguese poet and painter, had created a range of heteronyms, among them the black guerrilla fighter Mutimati Barnabé João, author of *We, the People*, a poetic pamphlet that excited and agitated the febrile days of independence in Mozambique. *As Quibíricas* begins where *The Lusiads* leaves off, and shares exactly the same structure and the same number of lines as Camões's work. As for the pirate edition of *Luuanda*, what makes it interesting is not only its artifice, but most of all its perversity. It was published by an agent of the political police in Portugal, in 1965, taking advantage of the scandal that resulted from Luandino Vieira – then locked up in Tarrafal Prison for seeking to create a bomber network – being awarded the Grand Literature Prize of the Portuguese Writers' Association. A note in the book asserts that it was printed in Belo Horizonte, in the Brazilian state of Minas Gerais, a piece of false information, of course, but the only way of justifying its circulation at a time when Portuguese publishers were forbidden from publishing it.

I never managed to forget Alberto Caeiro. From time to time I would pull him away from the company of Luandino Vieira and Frey Ioannes Garabatus and reread him. I realized the delusion had defeated me when I quoted one of the fake lines, believing it to be one of his real ones, among a group of his fans. It was at precisely that moment, as the poet's devotees tormented me with anxious questions, and I stammered evasions, trying to avoid a ludicrous admission that I had quoted an apocryphal line, that I decided to go all the way. I needed to find out who had written this book.

Months went by. In March 2001 I travelled to São Paulo to visit José Mindlin's library, a pilgrimage compulsory for anybody with an interest in our language. I left with my heart pounding, having leafed through two copies of *The Lusiads*, from 1572, one with the figure of the pelican, on the frontispiece, turned to the right, and the other with the same figure turned to the left. Mindlin also showed me an original edition of the sonnets and songs of Petrarch; some of the lines, which criticized the papacy, had been covered in India ink by the censorship of the period. Time, however, had undertaken to erase the censorious ink, restoring the forbidden words to the future. That book would have gone well in my library. The state of euphoria in which I left gave me the courage to call a cab and give the driver an address I knew by heart:

"I'm going to Calçada de Eleguá, number fifteen."

The man hesitated. Thirty-four years on the job and he'd never heard of such a place. Did I know which neighborhood it was in? No, I didn't know anything, apart from the street name, and it was possible the street wasn't even called that anymore, but I was willing to give him a generous tip if he managed to find it. It took us the rest of the afternoon. Night had already launched itself, strident and glowing, over the vast city, when the taxi dropped me outside a low, drab building, on a crookedly paved sidewalk. I rang the doorbell but no sound announced my presence. I knocked on the door, lightly at first, then with some force, and finally with no hope at all, and it was only then that it opened.

The dark stare, the thick hand, with dirty nails, holding the door – no, that wasn't what I'd been expecting. To tell the truth, I don't know what I'd been expecting. I think I was expecting a miracle, in the form of a thin ghost, bent-shouldered, hat on his head, round glasses, a ridiculous white mustache. Everything about this fellow before me, however, was real and rough.

"May I ask what it is you want?"

Books, I told him. Old books and papers. Somebody had told me a publishing house used to operate at this address once upon a time, and I wanted to know whether there might still be a few books forgotten around the place. I told him I worked for a secondhand bookstore and that I paid well for old books and papers. The man shook the torpor off his shoulders. He smelled of alcohol.

"Publisher? It was a doctor who used to live here. An English doctor. Died some time back."

He opened the door a bit further and only then did I notice that he was bare-chested, in shorts and sandals, and that he had a trident tattooed on his chest. Inside everything was dark and untidy. Yes, he said with some effort, dragging his voice out, there were books. There were papers. His mother, Dona Inácia, had worked for the doctor for thirty-five years, cleaning house, making his meals, taking care of the old man in his final days, and when he died he'd left her everything. The books he'd stored away himself years earlier, in a yard, where they were protected from the rain.

"Want to see?"

I did. I was determined to follow my mistake through, all the way. I trailed the man through the ruins. The floor, with wooden floorboards, had given way in a few places. The roof was, likewise, not in the best condition. Dampness slid down the walls, between the spider webs and some pale kind of flora, and with it came a strong smell of dead things. The yard, what he called the yard, was no more than a small patio wedged between high walls. In one of the corners there stood a precarious construction, made of wood, with a zinc roof, which looked to me like a chicken coop. It was full of books. I picked one at random. *Panic*, by Anthony Moraes. Poetry. The design for the cover, simple, elegant, was exactly like that for *Cata-*

log of Shadows, the only difference being that on Anthony Moraes's volume, there was a small long-legged bird sitting in the bottom right-hand corner, in the place of the publisher's name. I shivered.

"OK," I said. "How much do you want for the lot?"

I returned the following morning accompanied by a friend, Kelly Araújo, a professor of African history, who agreed to keep the books in her apartment, without even the slightest doubts about my motives. This time, the man had dressed up to receive us, in a light suit, or a suit that had once been light, and he was chattier. He told us that the English man, Mr. Carlos Roberto, yeah, just like the singer Roberto Carlos but the other way around, had died in 1970 from heart trouble, and had been buried in a cemetery nearby. I wanted to know if he'd lived alone that whole time.

"He never married? He didn't have girlfriends?"

The man looked at me, looked at Kelly, and lowered his voice:

"Oh no, no, he wasn't that kind of person, senhor, no. Dr. Carlos Roberto was a very serious man, very respectful. My mother used to say, Dr. Carlos Roberto could never fall into sin, not even in his thoughts."

I counted thirty copies of *Catalog of Shadows*, by Alberto Caeiro; twenty-three of *Panic*, by Anthony Moraes, a Luso-Chinese man from Hong Kong, according to how he was introduced in a brief note on the back cover; and there was also a volume of stories, *All*

About God, authored by a São Paulo man of Italian heritage called Francisco Boscolo, as well as a large number of English and Brazilian magazines.

"And what about letters? Didn't he leave any letters?"

The man looked at me in mute astonishment. I explained that a lot of people showed up at secondhand bookstores looking for antique correspondence. Some letters, confessions by poets to their editors, for example, could be worth quite a bit of money once both correspondents have died. I said this as I handed him a pair of hundred-real notes. The man's face opened up with a flash of light. Yes, there were letters, but his good mother, Dona Inácia, had taken them with her. She had also taken some books. Dona Inácia had returned to the village of her birth, in the Bahian basin, not wanting to die in São Paulo, far from her nieces and nephews, from her cousins, far from the great peace of her childhood, and she had taken some of the Englishman's belongings with her, as if they'd been relics. Occasionally she sent news. He didn't know his mother's land himself, but he showed me an envelope he had received not long ago:

> *Inácia Assunção*
> *Nossa Senhora do Silêncio*
> *Cachoeira – Bahia*

The following day, a Saturday, I was already on a plane bound for Salvador, and a few hours later I got off a bus in the town of Cachoeira. Night was drawing in. A horizontal golden light was beaming against the old walls. The people, the dogs, even the birds, were moving slowly, as if all trapped in the same honey. I rented a room at the Carmo, a former convent now a small hotel, I put on my bathing suit and went for a swim in the pool. There were no other guests. That night somebody took me to a Candomblé ceremony. All I remember is the nervous din of the atabaque hand-drums, growing, growing, ever growing, and the women spinning in a joyful trance. As I was leaving, I was approached by a thin man, with an impertinent mustache, who took me by the arm, introduced himself, "I'm Alexandre," and without my asking him a thing said he was willing to take me to Nossa Senhora do Silêncio for just fifty reals.

"Here to Silêncio, that's thirty miles, old man, but it's been raining the last few days and the road's bad. Going and coming, it'll take some time. Best allow plenty of time for it. Wait for me at the hotel. I'll be there at eight."

It was exactly seven fifty-five when Alexandre walked into the hotel restaurant (I was drinking a papaya juice) and sat down next to me. He broke open a white bread roll, spread it generously with butter, then with honey and jam, and ate it. He poured himself some

47

café-com-leite, added two spoons of sugar, and sipped the hot drink slowly. Only then did he seem to notice me:

"So what's up, José?! Sleep well? Ladybug is out there, she can't wait to take you for a spin."

Ladybug was an old Harley-Davidson. In an earlier incarnation it must undoubtedly have been a powerful vehicle. There was still a certain nobility to it, the same arrogance with which Cachoeira's big old colonial mansions scorned the very idea of death, and that moved me. I climbed onto that mechanical dinosaur, and entrusted my soul to the Creator. Alexandre proved to be an optimist. The road was in a bad state, it's true, in those places where there was a road at all. A good part of the journey, however, we had to do cross-country, down sandy tracks hacked through barbed wire vegetation. No car ever could have made it through there.

Nossa Senhora do Silêncio – Our Lady of Silence. It does justice to its name. I think everybody monitored our arrival from a good half an hour in advance, the curves, the skids, the hesitations, just by the din of the motor. I found Dona Inácia seated by the door to her house, upright and solemn as a queen, while a happy brood of chicks cheeped and pecked around her skirts. The skin of her face, smooth and black, shone. Her hair, which was of an impossible brilliance, she wore in two long braids. Her eyes were lively and teasing. She looked straight at me with no surprise.

"I've been expecting your visit, young man, thirty years I've been expecting you. The doctor said you'd come. You should know I won't be selling you anything, I'm not selling, and I'm not letting you take any papers away from here. But if you want to look, well, fine, you can look."

She went into the house and returned minutes later with two shoeboxes filled with papers, which she put down on the sand. The shade of a mango tree sweetened the air. There was a bench up against the trunk. I sat down on it, lifted one of the boxes onto my lap and opened it. I don't know how long I spent there. Alexandre brought me a Coke and disappeared. I tried it, it was hot. Minutes later, or several hours, a girl walked over to me bringing soup. Finally I looked up and my eyes met Dona Inácia's. I showed her the photograph of a thin man, in a garden, an open book in his hands.

"This is the gentleman who was Charles Robert Anon?"

"Carlos Roberto, yes, my boss . . ."

"Did he speak Portuguese well?"

"Very well, he spoke very well, but with a heavy accent. Right up to the very end he always spoke with a heavy English accent – like you, senhor."

I sighed. I have a heavy Portuguese accent. I took another photo from the first box. A tall, strong old man, with a mustache and white goatee, a huge pipe in his hands, was looking straight ahead, staring fixedly, into the lens. He looked like a circus hypnotist posing on a poster. The picture must have been taken in the same garden, maybe the same afternoon, as the previous one.

"And this fellow – who's he?"

"That's Dr. Aleister." Dona Inácia spoke firmly. I only saw him twice but I never forget eyes like that, oh no. Who could? He was a foreigner and he didn't know a word of Portuguese. He and Dr. Carlos Roberto only ever talked in that language of you people. I didn't understand a word of it."

Alexandre reappeared with a tall, slender young woman in an airy dress, which the light seemed to dissolve. She had flowers on her dress and in her hair. She laughed at me, a humid laugh, and Alexandre scolded her, pretending to be angry. Then he pointed toward the east and I saw the darkness closing over the gorse. My time had come to an end. In just a few hours there would be no more light. I handed the boxes back to Dona Inácia and told her I would be back soon. Her eyes sparkled with mockery. I wanted to know, in one final throw of the dice, whether the old lady had read the letters herself and what she thought of the whole thing. What was her opinion of Mr. Charles Robert?

"I don't have opinions," she answered. "I just am."

The sky had gone out by the time we reached the main road. Alexandre lit the headlights. I believe he was driving by pure instinct. I could see, head spinning, the sharpened blades of the bramble bushes, the white sand thread of the path, the dark abyss and the stars, and then all of this at the same time. I was still so dazed by what I had read that at no point was I scared.

"How do you know this is the way?"

"I don't," he shouted. "We'll find out when we arrive."

When we arrived I gave him the fifty reals. Then I gave him another fifty. Then I invited him for dinner. I explained that I would be coming back to Cachoeira soon and asked him, if possible, to keep our trip to Nossa Senhora do Silêncio secret.

The next day, in São Paulo, I told Kelly what I'd found, I told her everything from the beginning, as I'm telling you now, from that afternoon when Pedro Rosa Mendes waved a small volume called *Catalog of Shadows* under my nose, up to the moment when I lifted a shoebox filled with old papers onto my lap. Even I was starting to disbelieve what I was saying. In one of the boxes, I told her, there were a number of letters signed by Aleister Crowley, the English occultist who visited Fernando Pessoa in Lisbon, in the summer of 1930; that visit ended, as we know, very bizarrely, with Fernando Pessoa and some friends staging Crowley's suicide – the man, they insisted, had thrown himself into the Boca do Inferno chasm in

Cascais. In a letter addressed to Charles Robert Anon, dated December 1936, Aleister Crowley recalls the episode, recounting it as an amusing anecdote, mocking the Portuguese police and the agents of Scotland Yard sent to Lisbon to solve the mystery. "It was a ridiculous death," he admits. And then he adds, straight afterward: "Whereas yours, being so prosaic, proved much more convincing; it proved, more than anything, convenient." Finally, before signing off, he asks Anon urgently to send him "some pounds." In another letter, two weeks later, he once again asks for money, adding that he had spent more than anticipated on the English documents he'd sent to Lisbon.

Kelly laughed, doubtful, just as I myself had laughed when I'd first seen a copy of *Catalog of Shadows*. Seeing how serious I looked, however, she was startled. In January 2002, she agreed to accompany me to Salvador. We went prepared, with a good digital camera for photographing documents and a good-quality recorder. At the Carmo Hotel, in Cachoeira, nobody knew a thing about Alexandre. As had happened the previous time, it was he who found us. He showed up at the hotel, at breakfast, two days after our arrival:

"You're late, old man. Dona Inácia's already gone."

"Gone?"

"Yeah – passed on. She asked me to give you this."

He opened a leather folder and took out the photograph of

Charles Robert Anon, in a garden, a book open in his hands. On the back of the photo, the same one I'd seen before in Nossa Senhora do Silêncio, somebody had written in pencil in a childish hand: "Father Dionísio."

I shook my head, baffled:

"Father Dionísio?!"

"I was a boy, but I remember him, yeah, he was here several times. We've got some of the oldest Candomblé houses in Brazil right here in Cachoeira."

I shrugged. And?

"Father Dionísio – you don't know about him? – he was a great medium. He started coming here, to the Spiritism Center, and then got interested in Candomblé and those other Macumba religions. He became one of their priests. Then he died and became an *entidade* spirit. I even know a Macumba chant . . ."

Alexandre raised his voice to a falsetto:

> "Here comes Father Dionísio
> Here he comes, here he comes
> with his four shadows
> all paving the way:
> Caeiro, Seu Álvaro, Reizinho, and Pessoa.
> Here comes Father Dionísio, everyone!

prepare the wine,
the blessing, dear father
– oh, my good people!"

Kelly started to laugh. This time I laughed with her. I roared with laughter, convulsing, till tears had sprung from my eyes, and I went on laughing, unable to control myself, while Alexandre just shook his head.

"Oh," he said, "I don't know. I reckon the Exu spirit's not far away."

Elevator Philosophy

HARDLY ANYBODY notices me. People don't see me. They just whisper "Fifth floor" or "Fourteenth" in my direction, and then they forget all about me. Invisibility is a matter of practice, like swallowing swords. Incidentally, my friend, the fact I mention sword-swallowing isn't random. I know what I'm talking about. Before I was a lift operator I worked forty-five years in a circus. I learned to swallow swords, fire, shards of glass, scorpions, even barbed wire. With practice, a man can swallow anything. I was getting ready to innovate in the act, I was going to be the first artiste to swallow firearms and explosives, grenades, sticks of dynamite, pistols, possibly machine-guns, when I started feeling bad, real bad, this sharp pain in the epigastrium, violent nausea, and I discovered I had a stomach ulcer. I quit the circus.

It was Brave Hugo the lion tamer, who got me this job. I found it a bit tough at first. You see, the thing is, I'd gotten used to wandering. I mean, circus folk, we're kind of gypsies, *multivagos*, as Amazing

Mandrake the magician liked to say, one day we were in the big city, in a potent, animated metropolis, and the next we were nowhere. I was born in the circus. My mother was a contortionist. Emília, The Marvelous Snake-Woman. My father was Jolly Bignose, the poor clown. When I was nine years old, Jolly Bignose ran away with the Astonishing Jean-Pierre, the wire-walker, dragged off by a crazy love that nobody had ever suspected, and from which my mother never recovered. Emília grew very thin. She spent her days twisting, contorting herself, practicing new positions. She would tie herself up, to the point where she couldn't untangle herself on her own and I'd have to help her, and I would often despair, and I could see myself trying to snip her with a pair of pruning shears, a knee here, an elbow there, in order, at last, to straighten her out. She would get straightened out, but she could barely stay upright. A few years ago, I took her to a clinic. They did a number of x-rays on her. The doctor took me aside and showed me one of the plates:

"You see?"

I turned the picture around in my hands, concerned.

"No, doctor, I don't see anything!"

"Precisely," replied the doctor. "There's nothing to see. Your mother no longer has any bones. Not a one to be seen. None. They've gone, dissolved. It's an extreme case of osteoporosis."

You see? Osteoporosis. And people called it talent.

As for my father, I saw him again, after many years had passed, in a wretched circus in Afogados da Ingazeira in the northeast of Brazil. By that point he had lost the Bignose and everyone just called him The Clown. Everyone in this case was very few people. The quality of a circus can be measured in the extent and brilliance of the names of its performers. My father's final circus boasted only a clown – him – and a wire-walker, Pierre. My father also performed in the skin-and-bone of Ulio, the thinnest-man-in-the-world, a new act, whose authenticity impressed me. Pierre, meanwhile, was multiplied into two other characters: Tarzan, the chameleon-tamer, and Bruna, a tap dancer. Trading in the lions for chameleons was a bold, clever choice, I thought, especially because it reduced expenses on food and transportation of the animals. Unfortunately there didn't seem to be any audience with an interest in watching a chameleon act, or at least not in Afogados da Ingazeira. People think it's more exciting watching a man stick his head in the mouth of a lion, than sticking the head of a chameleon into his own. As somebody who got used to putting all kinds of dangerous objects in my mouth, I thought different.

My first job, when I was still a child, was washing the elephants. An arduous task, not least because ours, of which there were three, were all more than half a century old and had wrinkles so deep that the brushes would disappear into them. I then moved on to become assistant to The Infallible Red-Beard, the knife-thrower, until the day I lost my right ear. Swallowing swords seemed less of a risk. It was the Amazing Mandrake who taught me the trade and gave me my stage name: Aladdin the Incredible.

The Amazing Mandrake, poor thing, disappeared right in the middle of a performance. He got into a box, sitting atop The Exceptionally Rare White Tiger, and we never saw him again. Not him or the tiger. You can't imagine how much work it was painting that tiger. We'd thought about a white elephant first, but we didn't have the budget for the paint. There were two boxes. They would get into one and re-appear in the other. But this time the Exquisite Pocahontas opened the first box and – nothing. She opened the second – nothing. We broke both boxes apart with hammers . . . nothing. Neither the Exceptionally Rare White Tiger, nor the Amazing Mandrake. They disappeared forever. One night I dreamed about them. The Amazing Mandrake atop the Exceptionally Rare White Tiger, journeying between the stars. The Amazing Mandrake turned to me, smiled (he was a gentleman with a radiant smile), and said: "The stars are the final road for the *multivagos*."

This elevator is my world now. At least I'm still moving. I never stop. I'm still a *multivago* only now I'm a vertical one. I corrected my name to Ascension, which, in view of my role, feels more suitable than Aladdin the Incredible. Sometimes, when I'm in a more pessimistic mood, I contemplate switching to Descension, but my bitterness, thank God, is a shadow that always passes quickly.

Invisibility has its advantages. I hear a lot of conversations. I see strange things. I'm coming to the conclusion that the world out there is not much different from a circus. There are rich clowns and poor clowns. Tamers of wild beasts, cracking whips at vegetarian tigers, with pre-recorded roars to frighten the throng but which in reality are so fearful that even a cockroach scares them. There are the tightrope-walkers and the contortionists. The ones always sitting on the fence, and those lacking a spine. There are the ones who pull rabbits out of top hats, and those who themselves disappear along with the rabbits, and the top hats, and all the money of the just.

The circus is the world condensed. Like condensed milk – kind of artificial, but much sweeter. Us folk learn to laugh. Learn to laugh to combat the pain.

The Dog Charmer

Eliseu Capitango likes dogs. He ended up owning more than twenty, all trained to hunt partridges. He used to sell them at the Bailundo market, on the Praça Nova, to people who lived in remote rural villages. The farmers would take the gundogs away with them, pleased because from that day on they would have partridges for dinner, if not every night then at least once or twice a week. Some days later, depending how far the village, the dogs would reappear at Eliseu's house. He would wait a week and then sell them again. Some would appear at his door with partridges in their mouths.

One of the gundogs, Maroto, showed up one afternoon leading a herd of goats (seven of them, to be exact). Capitango killed one of the animals and sold the rest. The next morning, he was in the yard, roasting the blessed goat, when his wife called him over. It was a sun-drenched Sunday, all the more of a Sunday for being so joyfully sunny. On the front porch, twisting his dense moustache with thick, impatient fingers, stood the guy to whom he had sold Maroto. The dog charmer didn't recognize him right away because the man who had bought the gundog had been dressed in severe black, like a priest, and this man was now in uniform and seemed taller and more solid. Capitango shuddered when he saw the stars gleaming on his shoulders. He stood to attention:

"Good day, general. To what do I owe the honor of a visit from you? Have you come to buy another dog?"

Letting go of his moustache, the soldier pointed an accusing finger at him:

"You told me you trained dogs to catch partridges. But what you really do is teach them to steal little goats!"

Eliseu Capitango shrank back. He was physiologically horrified by high-ranking officers. You really could call it an allergy. When he found himself face to face with a general, with a brigadier, and even, on some occasions, a simple lieutenant, Capitango had felt his stomach expand, his guts come undone, and he struggled to contain his wind. The first fart exploded like a firecracker in the bleached-white light of the morning, causing the general to recoil by a couple of steps, alarmed, indignant, unnerved:

"What the devil?!"

There followed another ferocious burst. The general brought his hand to his gun, readying himself for combat:

"That is a declaration of war, Senhor Capitango, a major offensive!"

Eliseu Capitango made his apologies. He'd eaten something really spoiled the night before, either that or, who knows, maybe it was something more serious, one of those illnesses that were highly contagious, like Ebola or Marburg. The general retreated another two steps. He shielded his nose with a handkerchief.

"Are there other sick people here in the house?" he asked, his voice cracking.

"Oh, yes, we're all like this."

The soldier backed away, tripping over his own fear. He got into his car and ordered the driver to beat a rapid retreat. He never came back. Could have been worse.

When I met him, Eliseu Capitango was still casting spells on dogs. He swore to me, however, that he had given up the lucrative deception of selling the same gundog an infinite number of times. Firstly, the episode with the general had frightened him. Secondly, he had gotten old. As so often happens, he had turned honest not out of repentance but out of fear and fatigue:

"Lying was exhausting. I had to remember all the people I'd sold dogs to, so as not to sell them the same one again a few days later."

I asked him how he'd managed to seduce the creatures. He told me he communicated with them through smells. He managed to emit corporeal odors that the dogs could interpret, the way a person reads a book. He had learned the trick by himself as a child. He'd spent years developing it.

"Seriously?" I was amazed. "That's something you can practice?"

"Oh yes, sir, that you can. But you need the gift. You can't teach a donkey to fly."

Depending on the strength and direction of the wind, he was able to communicate with dogs at some considerable distance. He sent the packs on the hunt for partridges. With any luck they would also bring him rabbits. For years, communication had happened in one direction only – Capitango sending his olfactory messages, which the gundogs interpreted. In recent months, however, he had been training his sense of smell, so that he might read the messages from the dogs, too. I didn't believe him:

"That's not possible!"

Capitango smiled. He shut his eyes. Focused. Seconds later, a large, self-assured dog, with big, intelligent eyes, appeared next to us.

"This is Maroto," said Capitango. "The one who stole the goats. He likes you, but not the smell of your pants. You've got cats, haven't you?"

I nodded confirmation. A lot of cats. I live surrounded by cats. So that's what it was, Eliseu went on, my clothes smelled of cats, and Maroto, like almost all dogs, hated cats. I said goodbye to the old man with a solemn hug and left. I've never had cats. I hate cats, every bit as much as Maroto does. I agreed with the dog charmer so as not to hurt him. I don't doubt that Capitango has discovered some way of talking chemically with his dogs. He just needs a little more practice.

The Night They Arrested Santa Claus

O LD PASCOAL had a magnificent, long, white beard, which tumbled stormily down his chest. Fashion? No, merely dilapidation. But it was because of that beard that he was able to get work. Because of that, and because he had been born an albino, with little blinking pink eyes that were always hidden behind a huge pair of dark glasses. In those days he was no longer even thinking about getting a job, convinced he would soon die on the streets of the city – from sadness, from hunger. He was living off the soup he was given daily by the General, and the occasional crust of bread he found in the dumpsters. At night he'd sleep in the bar, on the billiard table, rolled up in a blanket, another favor from the General, and he would dream about the swimming pool.

He had worked as a caretaker at the swimming pool for forty years – since its very first day. He knew how to read, to count, as well as all the devotions he'd learned at the Mission, and that was not to mention his honesty, his good hygiene, his love of work. The whites liked him, it was always Pascoal this, Pascoal that, they entrusted their small children to him, some of them even invited him to play football (he was a good goalie), others confided in him, asked to borrow his bedroom for their romantic encounters.

Pascoal's room was right next to the men's changing rooms. That was his home. The whites clapped him on the back:

"Pascoal, the only black Angolan who has a house with a pool!"

They'd laugh:

"Pascoal, the whitest black man in Africa."

They'd tell jokes about albinos:

"Do you know the one about the local chief who on The Day of the Portuguese Race was invited to give a speech? The guy got up on the podium, cleared his throat, and began: *Here in Angola we're all Portuguese, whites, blacks, mulattos and albinos, all Portuguese.*

The blacks, on the other hand, did not like Pascoal. The women tutted, they spat when he passed, or, worse still, pretended they didn't even see him. The kids would jump the wall, really early in the morning, and throw themselves into the pool. He had to get up, in his underpants, to chase them out. One day he bought a rifle with rubber pellets, secondhand, and started firing at them from his hiding place behind the acacias.

When the Portuguese fled the country, Pascoal understood that his happy days had come to an end. He witnessed the arrival of the guerrilla warriors with displeasure, and the gunshots, and the plundering of the houses. What he found hardest, in the months that followed, was to see them going into the pool. Comrade this, comrade that, as if nobody had a name anymore. The kids, the same ones Pascoal had previously driven out with pellet shots, peed from the diving boards. Until one afternoon there was no water. It didn't come back the next day, nor the next, nor ever again. The chlorine ran out soon afterward. The swimming pool withered. It turned yellow, a dull yellow, and then suddenly it was filled with frogs. At first, Pascoal tried to fight off the invasion with his rifle. The plan didn't work. The more frogs he killed, the more appeared. Happy, huge frogs, and on nights when the moon was full they would sing into the small hours, muffling the echo of the gunshots, in the distance, and the barking of the dogs.

A tiredness fell over the houses and the city began to die. Africa – let's call it that – once again took hold of what it had formerly possessed. They dug wells in backyards. They lit bonfires in the gardens. The grass broke through the asphalt, invaded the sidewalks, the walls, the patios. Women piled corn in great halls. Refrigerators began to be used for storing shoes. Pianos made excellent rabbit hutches. Generations of goats grew up eating libraries – erudite goats, some specializing in French literature, others in finance or architecture. Pascoal emptied the swimming pool, cleaned it, got together all the money he had and bought chickens. He asked the pool to forgive him:

"My friend," he said, "it's only for a few months. I'm going to sell eggs, I'll sell the chicks and buy some good water, I'll buy chlorine, you'll go back to being as beautiful as you used to be."

The times that followed, however, were even worse. One afternoon, soldiers showed up and took the chickens away. Pascoal said nothing. He should, perhaps, have said something.

"The albino's acting real full of himself." One of the soldiers got annoyed. "Probably thinks he's white, check him out, little white phony."

They beat him. They left him for dead in the pool. Months later, more soldiers came. They'd been told there was an albino there who raised chickens, and since they didn't find any, of course, they beat him too.

The war returned with a fury. Planes bombed the city, what was left of it, for fifty-five days. On day thirty-six, one of the bombs destroyed the swimming pool. For weeks Pascoal walked, adrift, among the debris.

One day three men showed up in a jeep, one white, one mulatto, one black, all of them in jackets and ties.

"Oh God, oh God!" wailed the mulatto, waving his hand in a broad gesture of dismay. "It's been an urbicide, an urbicide . . ."

Pascoal didn't know what that word meant, but he liked it. "It was an urbicide," he repeated, and to this day, whenever he remembers the swimming pool, he spends hours chewing over that phrase: "it was an urbicide, an urbicide." A troop of extremely foreign whites, all in little blue hats, picked him up early one rainy morning and brought him to Luanda. He spent two days in the hospital, where he was treated for his injuries and given food. Then they sent him away. The old man started to live on the street. One day – it was December and very hot – the Indian man from the new supermarket, in Mutamba, came over to talk to him:

"We need a Santa Claus," he said. "With you we can save on the beard, and besides, since you've got that whole Nordic look, the thing seems more authentic. We're paying three million a day. Would that work for you?"

His job was to stand outside the supermarket, dressed in red pajamas, with a hat on his head. Since he was very skinny, he needed to have two pillows tied to his belly. The heat made Pascoal suffer, he sweated all day long under the sun, but for the first time in many years he felt happy. Dressed like that, with a sack in his hand, he would offer gifts to the little children (condoms donated by a Swedish NGO to the Ministry of Health) and invited the parents

71

into the store. "I am the *Cambulador* Santa Claus," he explained to the General.

A cambulador had been a job in Angola until the first half of the century: people hired them to entice customers to the door of their commercial establishments. Pascoal liked the job more and more every day. The children would run to him with open arms. The women would laugh, complicit, they'd wink at him (no woman had ever smiled at him); the men would greet him deferentially:

"Good afternoon, Santa Claus! How are we doing for presents this year?"

The old man particularly enjoyed the amazement of the street kids. They gathered in a circle around him. They begged for permission to touch the sack. One of them, a very little, scrawny one, hung on to his pants:

"Mr. Santa," he begged, "give me a balloon?"

Pascoal was under strict instructions to give condoms only to accompanied children, and even then it depended on what their company looked like. The deal was very clear: street kids were to be swatted away.

At the end of the second week, when the store shut, Pascoal decided not to take off his disguise and he returned to the bar in that outrageous get-up. The General saw him and said nothing. He served him his soup in silence.

"There's such poverty in this country," the old man complained as he sipped his soup. "Crime does pay."

That night he didn't dream about the swimming pool. He saw a very beautiful lady descending from the sky and coming to rest on the edge of the billiard table. The lady was wearing a long dress with little shiny stones and a golden crown on her head. The light burst from her skin like a lamp.

"You are Santa Claus," the lady said to him. "I sent you here to help the lost children. Go to the store, put the toys in the sack, and hand them out to the kids."

The old man awoke in a sort of daze. In that thick night, a glowing dust was floating all around the billiard table. He rolled himself back up in his blanket but he couldn't fall asleep again. He got up, put on his Santa Claus clothes, picked up his sack, and went out. Soon he was in Mutamba. The store was dazzling, huge in the deserted square, like a flying saucer. The Barbies occupied the main window, each in her own dress but all with the same bored smile. In the other window were the mechanical monsters, the plastic guns, the electric toy cars. Pascoal knew that if he broke the glass of this window display, he would be able to put his hand through between the bars and open the door. He picked up a stone and broke the glass. He was already just about to leave, with his sack totally full, when a police officer appeared. That same moment, behind him, an acacia lit up, on the corner, and Pascoal saw the Lady, smiling at him, floating over the blazing flowers. The police officer didn't seem to notice a thing.

"Shameless old degenerate," he shouted. "You gonna tell me what you got in that sack?"

Pascoal felt his mouth opening, without his intending it, and he heard himself say:

"Roses, officer."

The police officer looked at him, confused.

"Roses? Whoah, the old man's lost it . . ."

He gave him a hard slap with the back of his hand. He took his gun out of its holster, pointed at his head, and shouted:

"Roses, are they? Show me these roses, then! . . ."

The old man hesitated a moment. Then he looked once again at the acacia in flower, and again saw the Lady smiling at him, so very beautiful, a whole carnival of light. He took the sack and tipped it out at the police officer's feet. They really were roses – plastic ones.

But roses all the same.

The Trap

JUSTO MARTÍRIO looked suspiciously at the façade. In another time it might have been a very stately building. The imposing marble entrance and the art deco stained-glass door, what was left of it, still retained traces of a lost grandeur. The lawyer consulted the diary in which he had made a note of the number – 139, 9B – shook his head, and with a sigh of defeat walked in. He had returned to Luanda two months earlier, after twenty-five years of exile in Lisbon, and he still had not resigned himself to just how decrepit the city was. In the first days he would get back home totally wrung out, fill the bathtub with hot water, undress, and lie down in it to cry. He hadn't made a single friend since his arrival. On weekdays he worked from eight to eight. On weekends he would visit his sister, Julieta, who was personal secretary to the Minister of Trade. His sister lived alone. She had no children. The lawyer hesitated a moment, as his eyes got accustomed to the gloom. A thin fellow, dressed in a very dirty, very worn military jacket, emerged from the shadows and positioned himself in front of him like an exclamation point.

"Where are you going?"

Justo Martírio noticed that the man was missing the thumb on his right hand. Only then did he see the bunch of keys. He sighed even more deeply. His sister didn't like hearing him sigh like that. She got annoyed:

"It's like you hate this country," she would say. "You people, the people who jumped ship, you have so much bitterness in your hearts."

It wasn't bitterness. Only sadness. And yes, he had jumped ship. He'd jumped ship because he knew how to swim. Many of those who had stayed behind on the ship would have gone, too, if they could. Now they watched the return of those who had jumped, those who hadn't spent months on end eating nothing but grilled swordfish with rice, those who hadn't taken bucket baths, those who couldn't identify a gun by the sound of a shot, those who had never known the humiliation of standing in lines, or of water shortages, they watched their return and did not forgive them. Who was it, after all, that had so much bitterness in their hearts? He thought about all this whenever his sister provoked him. Yet he kept quiet. He didn't like arguing.

"Ninth floor . . ."

The man inserted one of the keys into the slot next to the elevator door, and right away a light started to blink. The elevator came down.

"It's got to be this way," he explains. "Otherwise they destroy everything. But you can rest easy, old man, the elevator's got its own generator. Even if the power goes out across the whole city, it'll keep working. It never stops. It's the ninth floor you're going, you're sure?"

Justo Martírio confirmed this. The man opened the door, put the key into the slot corresponding to the ninth floor, and said goodbye:

"Have a good day."

The door closed, the elevator shuddered and began to rise, panting heavily, struggling, like an asthmatic animal. Justo Martírio had the sensation that he was regressing, rising endlessly, toward the primordial chaos. Looking through the splintered glass, he could see the slow floors passing and their confused universe of rust and ruin. With every floor, the devastation increased. Copper and plastic tubing climbed the walls, pierced the ceilings and multiplied, further up, in a muddle that was impossible to untangle. On the fifth floor he spotted bits of mechanical debris and naked children running among them. The sixth was plunged into a thick darkness. The seventh and eighth seemed abandoned. Then the elevator stopped and Justo Martírio stepped out, bewildered, into a clean, well-kept hallway, which seemed not to belong to the building, or to the city, or to their time. The doors, three of them, one on each wall, were protected by strong bars. A fourth grille, even broader and more solid than the others, painted impeccably in red, blocked access to the staircase. He noticed a metal plate screwed to the middle door. He walked over to it and read: "Gonçalves & Sons – Accountants." He'd probably gotten the number of the building wrong. He checked his diary again. That moment he heard a noise behind him, and when he turned around, startled, he understood that somebody had called the elevator. He saw it going down, a light sinking into the abyss, and only then remembered that he had no way of calling it again. He didn't have the keys. Alarmed now, his heart pounding, he rang the doorbell, but was answered only by silence. A piece of paper, postcard-shaped, taped to the door, caught his eye: "We are closed for the holidays – We reopen on August 1st." He looked at his watch. It was a Monday, July 6th, there were twenty-five days to go. He tried to open the grille that led to the stairs. Impossible. In addition to the lock, a steel chain linked by two enormous padlocks tied it to the doorpost in three tight loops.

Justo Martírio remembered the wicker traps with which, in his boyhood, he used to fish. The fish would find it easy to enter through the cone-shaped opening, which was narrow but elastic, at one end. Once they were inside, they couldn't get out again. Sometimes, if it took him a while to retrieve the traps, a bigger fish would get inside and eat the others.

Fortunately he had brought his cellphone. He could call somebody, explain the ridiculous situation he found himself in, and they could come to rescue him right away. He opened his case and took out the phone. What happened next is what finished him off. The lights went out and, at that moment, the phone slipped from his fingers. Justo Martírio could have kept still. He could have knelt down, calmly, and looked for the cellphone. Instead, however, he took two steps, flustered, seeking the support of a wall, and, with his second step, the cellphone was crushed.

He yelled. He punched the bars until his fists were injured. Finally, he sat down on the ground, and cried.

They're Not Like Us

'Tis true that Judas was a traitor, but with a lantern in his hand; he drew up his treachery in the dark, but carried it out quite in the open. The octopus, darkening, withdraws from others' sight, and the first treachery and theft it carries out is of the light itself, that its colors may not be seen.

—Father António Vieira

W HAT SAVED Dona Filipinha de Carpo that night was father António Vieira. The old lady had lain down to read the "Sermon to the Fishes" and had been so delighted by the Jesuit's words that at two in the morning she was still awake. That was how she came to hear, in Carolina's room, the stealthy creak of the window opening and then, no doubt about it, a man's footsteps. She got up in her nightdress (an amazing nightdress of patterned silk that Charles had brought her from Singapore) and made her way down the corridor, certain that something she had feared for years was happening at last. When she opened the door she saw a man leaning over the sleeping girl, she saw the knife, and she knew what was going to happen next.

"Don't do that," she said quietly, "she's only fifteen."

The man turned toward her and, pointing the knife at her, murmured:

"If you scream, we'll kill you right away!"

He was scared. Dona Filipinha felt sorry for him:

"Put the knife down," she said. "Put the knife down and we'll talk."

The man looked fierce but at the same time helpless. He was in an old army uniform, very worn, with open sandals revealing his painted nails, each a different color. He looked at her angrily:

"Talk? Talking doesn't take away our hunger!"

The old lady smiled.

"That's true! So let's go to the kitchen and I'll give you some hot soup. And then we can talk, if you want."

The man followed her, a grim expression on his face. In the kitchen, he sat down, put the knife on the table, and only then seemed to calm slightly.

"In Cuito," he said, "we used to dream about food every night."

Dona Filipinha was looking at him as she prepared the soup:

"You were in Cuito? . . ."

The man seemed not to hear her.

"That was before we started eating the dead. Now all our dreams are about them."

He picked up the knife and cut open a bread roll. He cut a big slice of cheese and put it on the bread. He ate the whole thing without taking a breath. Dona Filipinha put a plate of soup and a spoon down in front of him. He pushed the spoon away, picked up the plate with both hands and sipped the soup.

"If you'd been sleeping, we would have slit your throat. Yours and your daughter's."

Dona Filipinha refilled his plate.

"What's your name?"

The man shrugged:

"We don't have a name!"

There was a sound of gunshots from outside. An initial burst, very close, then another in the distance. A tired voice shouted something.

Then nothing.

"It's like that every night," the woman said. "Last week I found a dead body on the stairs. They'd cut off his fingers. I counted eight of them scattered around the floor. Someone said he was a bandit."

The man looked at his own hands as if they belonged to someone else. He picked up the spoon and ate the rest of the soup in silence. He talked as if he were alone.

"We were seminarists, but the seminary shut down. Then we

went off to teach on the national literacy days, and then they enrolled us into the armed forces. We fought in the war for twenty years. We killed so many, and so many of us died."

He turned to Dona Filipinha:

"There were so few of us left to talk about what it was like!"

He wiped his face and fell silent again. If he'd shut his eyes, one might have thought he was asleep. A bed creaked upstairs. A woman began to moan as the bed creaked. It was as if she was right there, bent over the kitchen table, tense and sweating, biting the sheets and moaning in time with the bed.

"Get us a bag," the man said. "We haven't got all night."

Dona Filipinha handed him a leather bag, wide and deep, and he stood, opened the drawers and started collecting up the silver cutlery. At that moment, Carolina came into the kitchen, totally naked, in the ridiculous splendor of her fifteen years. She stood there a moment under the light, blinking, like a gazelle surprised in its sleep:

"I've just come for a glass of milk," she said. "I didn't know there were people here."

Dona Filipinha pushed her away tenderly.

"Go back to your room, child. I'll bring you your milk in a moment."

The man shook his head:

"You shouldn't let her walk around like that. Not at times like these, not in this country."

The woman became distressed:

"She's still a child. She could be your daughter."

She said this without much conviction. When Carolina was twelve, Dona Filipinha had taken her out of the family home because her five brothers, all of them older than her, were taking advantage of her (her mother had said it was she who was taking advantage of them). Now she was watching her grow up beautiful, troubling, and she felt she was raising a carnivorous flower. She wanted to talk about something else, but nothing else came to mind.

"I'm afraid of her," she whispered. "She's not like us."

For the first time, the man looked her in the eye.

"This country isn't ours anymore either," he said, lowering his voice. "It's their country now. God abandoned us, and the world has forgotten us."

He put the bag down on the table:

"Do you have jewels?"

Dona Filipinha went to her bedroom to fetch the box in which she kept her jewels, opened it and emptied everything into the bag. Her voice trembled a little.

"I don't have anything else . . ."

The man pointed at the gold ring she had on the little finger of her left hand.

"That one, too!"

The woman sighed deeply, and looked straight at him.

"There's no way. It was a gift from my grandmother, who in turn inherited it from her mother. It's been in this family for four generations. This one stays with me."

The man grabbed hold of her hand and pulled off the ring. Then he slung the bag over his shoulder, walked out of the kitchen, opened the front door and left. Dona Filipinha waited for him to go down the stairs. Then she went back to the kitchen and poured a glass of milk. At that moment she heard a hubbub of voices outside, and people running, a quick burst of gunfire, laughter. Carolina, naked, was leaning out her bedroom window.

"Bad news!" she called inside. "They've taken out your friend!"

Dona Filipinha put the glass of milk onto the bedside table and sat down on the bed. She felt so tired.

"He wasn't my friend," she said. "And in any case, he was dead already."

K40

THIS IS the tale of Pedro Paulo de Noronha, better known by his nom de guerre, K40, the best shot in Angola. A man who even when going wrong never failed to hit the target.

I saw him once, briefly, on an occasion when a friend and I were looking for a beach, not far from the mouth of the Quanza. It was a Saturday afternoon, it must have been February, maybe March. We had managed to escape the traffic when the heavens opened in a sudden downpour. I remember, moments later, the damp glare of the sun sliding across the asphalt. Leandro, my friend, pointed at a wooden sign planted on the left-hand side of the road:

AFTER-THE-END FARM.

"That's Pedro Paulo de Noronha's farm. You know him? I think we've got to drive across quite a lot of it to get to the beach."

He stopped the jeep, and I jumped out and raised the gate. Then we made our way, slowly, down a small beaten-earth road that cut through the dense bush. There were cacti, tall candelabras, and in the distance, scattered baobabs.

"So who is this man?"

Leandro smiled:

"The correct question would be: who *was* this man?"

Pedro Paulo de Noronha was sitting, accompanied by his wife and son, at a broad table on a porch beneath a zinc-covered canopy. He wiped his lips, unhurriedly, on a paper napkin and only then did he get up to greet us. He was a lean, lithe fellow, his muscles well defined under his tanned skin. His eyes, luminous but elusive, avoided mine. He shook Leandro's hand, with no warmth. As for me, I received only a nod. From a large pot set in the middle of the table rose a lively, joyful scent of palm oil. Muamba chicken. There was a dish with cassava funje and another with corn funje. A pan, full of water, with a soup spoon. I felt hungry. Pedro Paulo de Noronha did not, however, invite us to join him. He answered my friend's questions with brief phrases. His voice was cold, or maybe not cold, merely distant:

"Go straight ahead. You'll come to a little thatched hut. Then you turn right, down a path of loose sand, careful for the jeep not to get stuck. Once you're there you'll be able to see the beach."

He sat back down.

"If the jeep gets stuck, I'll send someone down with the tractor."

His wife smiled at me. She must have been very beautiful. She was beautiful still, with the melancholy nobility of an exiled queen. The lad was bare-chested. He had inherited his mother's dreaming eyes and his father's sharp profile, as well as his disdain. We said goodbye and got into the jeep.

"Pedro Paulo de Noronha. The name really doesn't mean anything to you?!"

No, it didn't. Leandro stopped the jeep. The beach was not especially beautiful. A line of melancholy, wind-beaten coconut palms. Murky sand, with a lot of leaves and pieces of broken branches. The sea was dark and heavy, and reminded me of a nervous animal caught in a cage, kicking, at regular intervals, at the bars.

"They say you sometimes see crocodiles . . ."

"What?!"

"Crocodiles. Don't you know what crocodiles are?! The river, bro, the Quanza empties out just a few kilometers from here. The crocodiles get dragged down. Some manage to make their way back up. Others come along the coast. Seems they can survive quite a while in the salt water."

There was nobody on the beach. Leandro took off his shirt. Then his pants and his underpants. He put on a pink and green swimsuit printed with toucans and palm trees. He sat down on the sand, his eyes staring out into the distance, fixed on the turbulent sea.

"Pedro Paulo de Noronha, marksmanship champion. Silver medal at Seoul. He also went by the name K40. Remember him now?"

K40! I did remember the episode. In 1975, just a few months before independence, a young MPLA commander punched a Portuguese officer, knocking him to the ground. It was in a nightclub frequented by the colonial bourgeoisie, in Huambo, following some stupid quarrel. A beautiful mulatta girl. A lot of beer. The officer left, furious, vowing revenge, and he did indeed return, shortly after, at the head of a large group of soldiers. Somebody ran in to inform the commander: "There's like forty army guys out there. They're going to kill you!" The guy didn't even hesitate. He straightened up, pulled out a knife and, opening the door, faced the soldiery:

"Come on, then," he shouted. "I'll geld all forty of you!"

The women ran out, screaming. More people gathered. The night ended beautifully, hours later, amid hugs and toasting, laughter, gallons of beer, long live Angola and long live Portugal. Pedro Paulo de Noronha left the place with the mulatta girl, with his honor intact and that curious nom de guerre – K40. Next time anyone heard of him was at the Seoul Olympics. K40, now with a general's star, returned to Luanda a hero. Decorations. Speeches. Parties and parades. Soon afterward, however, some misfortune or other befell him and he disappeared again.

"He got arrested, didn't he?"

"Affirmative."

"What did he do?"

Leandro shrugged. They say he insulted the Minister of Defense, in front of a number of officers, during an argument about war materiel procurement. He was accused of insubordination. They also accused him of racist arrogance, of anti-patriotic behavior, and of being nostalgic for the colonial days. K40 spent three years in military prison. He came out a wreck. He was drinking heavily. He let his beard grow. He stopped talking to anybody. What saved him was his wife's pregnancy. On the day the boy was born he swore off drink. He went back to dreaming. With the aid of a group of officers, his former colleagues, he bought a large plot of land, close to the mouth of the Quanza, and thus After-the-End Farm was born.

Leandro sighed:

"The guy never picked up a gun again, but to a lot of people he's still one of the best shots in the world, the man who managed a silver medal at the Seoul Olympics. That's what fucked him up; poor guy, all that damn fame."

Then one morning, very early, a group of armed men came to the farm. At the head of the group was a short man, broad-shouldered, with blazing eyes and brusque movements, which contrasted with his way of speaking, a gentle Portuguese so delicate and sleek it seemed to have been stolen moments earlier from a seminarian. He was wearing black pants, very high-waisted, and an immaculately white shirt tucked into the pants. He presented himself with a lengthy bow before Pedro Paulo de Noronha.

"General, please do me the honor of kindly accepting the respectful greetings of your admirer Severino Diewell."

With no further ado, he explained why he had come:

"I have been asked to execute a difficult task. Indeed, execute is the very word. In this case, a man. I have nothing against him personally. I barely know him. Just business, sir, you understand me? In these fierce times we're living in, if a man grows his nails it's not just to play guitar, you know! The individual for executing, let us say, the executee, is a resident of this capital city of ours, living in a nice apartment, and he spends his afternoons sitting in his study, opposite the window, writing on a computer. The executee, a journalist of some merit, but that is beside the point, works as a rule between three and six p.m., after which he turns on the light and lowers the blinds. We have found a very tall building under construction, a few blocks from the apartment, such that the top of the building in question has a perfect view of the executee's study. We have also managed to obtain an excellent weapon, this fine Dragunov, brand new. All we need now is somebody who's a good shot. Well, sir, that was when I remembered you, General, you are just the person to carry out this most delicate task. It needs to be on the first shot, you understand? one perfect shot, between the eyes, so that the individual doesn't suffer and we don't run any risk of his escaping. A single shot, bzzzz!, and job done. Naturally, we pay very well . . ."

K40 jumped to his feet. He put the palm of his right hand to Diewell's throat. His voice was trembling with fury:

"I'm a soldier, you hear me?! I'm not a killer. I won't do it!"

"You will." Severino Diewell didn't move a muscle. His voice was coming out even softer now. "General, sir, you are going to come with me. My men will stay here. If you don't complete the task, if you don't do it well, your family will die. I'm very sorry. Those are the rules of the game."

K40 sat back down. He was livid:

"I'm not doing it!"

Severino Diewell sat down, too. He took a deep breath. He looked ready to explode:

"Oh, for fuck's sake, old man! Do I really need to tell you, you don't have a choice? . . ."

For a good five minutes, nobody moved. Diewell sitting opposite Pedro Paulo de Noronha, eye to eye, and around both of them, still standing, the armed men. In the background, sitting on a wide leather sofa, his wife, very upright, with the boy on her lap. Finally Severino Diewell broke the silence:

"Very well," he said. "Are you a betting man? I am. So I'll make you a bet. I'm sure, general, that you must have read, as I did when I was a boy, the story of William Tell. I'll give you this gun now, with one single bullet. We'll put your son outside there, about a hundred and fifty meters away, with an apple on his head. You hit the apple and I'll leave, I'll take my men with me and no one gets hurt. You miss and I'll kill you, sir, and your family. Same thing if you refuse."

"I've never heard such a stupid suggestion!" muttered Pedro Paulo de Noronha. "Besides, I don't have any apples . . ."

"You've got lemons. We can do it with lemons."

"What nonsense. There's no way the boy would be able to balance a lemon on his head . . ."

"Right. Well, then an orange. And oranges are actually bigger than apples, and besides, they're much easier to see. An orange is a perfect target."

They all went outside. They chose a white wall, the wall of a small tool store, at a considerable distance from the house, but visible from its veranda. They walked back in silence. The woman picked the boy up in her arms and handed him to her husband.

"Whatever happens, I'm not going to forgive you."

Severino Diewell accompanied the boy to the tool store, stood him up against the wall and then placed a good-sized orange on his head.

"Don't move," he told him. "You can count on your father. He's a great hero . . ."

He stood near the boy, some three meters away, with his pistol in his hand, in case he needed to help him die. He was very serious. The other men surrounded Pedro Paulo de Noronha. One of them loaded the Dragunov. He held it out, with a slight bow, to the general:

"Man, good luck!"

Pedro Paulo de Noronha weighed up the weapon. Holding it with his left hand, he raised his right into the air, assessing the humidity, the direction and strength of the wind. He brought the weapon up to his face, pointed at the orange, and then, in an abrupt movement, turned it toward Severino Diewell and fired. The bullet sliced through the man's right ear, ricocheted off the wall and tore through the orange. There was a brief moment of amazement. One of the men shouted:

"Damn! And on a one-two! . . ."

A second man lowered his gun and applauded eagerly. The others copied him. The child wiped his face, which was wet with juice, and started to cry. His mother ran to him. Severino Diewell walked slowly toward Pedro Paulo de Noronha. Blood spurted from his open ear, in a thick strand, coloring his very black skin and the brightness of his shirt red. He pulled the general aside by the arm and whispered in his ear:

"I think you missed, my dear general, but God hit the target for you." He sighed. "And who am I to contradict the purposes of God?"

Leandro finished recounting the episode. He got to his feet. He picked up his board, held it to his chest, and threw himself into the sea. I stayed put. I opened my backpack, picked out a roast beef sandwich, and ate it enthusiastically. I sat there watching Leandro playing with the waves. He was a good storyteller. His voice changed, and his posture, each time one of the characters entered the scene. Who could have told him this one? When he returned, shaking the water out of his hair, I asked the question:

"How do you know that story? I mean, like that, with so much detail . . ."

My friend looked straight at me:

"What do you think, bro? I was there!"

He Said His Name Was Darkness

H E SAID his name was Welema, a name that in Umbundu means Darkness. None of us answered him. Nobody laughed. We didn't have the nerve. This lad had an unpleasant way of licking his lips, and these little blinking, treacherous eyes that struggled to hold the afternoon glare. He asked if he could play with us, and, though there was no room for him, we said yes and one of us quit the field and went to sit on the sand, in the sparse green shade of a coconut palm.

You wouldn't have considered Darkness a good player were it not for his speed. We just watched him flash past, his rough hair the color of dry grass and his luminescent skin, which ten years later would be dotted with nocturnal stains and marks, like the peel of an overripe banana. At that time, however, Darkness was only eleven years old, like all of us, and his skin – I say again – shone in the sunlight, limpid and smooth, like the skin of the blond angels in the catechisms.

We continued to applaud the first four goals. At the fifth, however, we raised an eyebrow, sitting in the green shade of the coconut palm, and let out a noisy tut of contempt: "Finally!"

That was all. Nobody dared to question the goals. Something about him struck fear into us, though we couldn't have said exactly what. Yes, we talked about this later. We talked about it for years. Deep in those little eyes there lived a spider in its web. Or maybe it was that unpleasant way he had of running his tongue along his lips, "snake-like," as one of us recalled. Or even the too high-pitched voice, like a piece of chalk scratching across the slate. The lad would show up on Saturday afternoons, and he always won, whatever the game – football, marbles, bicycle races, dominoes, or arm-wrestling.

Darkness didn't argue, he didn't threaten. All he did was blink his eyes, run his tongue over his lips, and down our arms would go. He smiled: "I won again."

We met him again many years later. It wasn't hard to recognize him, notwithstanding the cruel baldness and that skin in such poor condition it looked like it had been stolen from a cadaver after a tough fight. I reckon we would have recognized him even if he'd changed race, sex – even football club! – because we once again felt that tightening in the stomach, that old torment, the moment he pierced us with the blazing sting of those little blinking eyes. He spoke first:

"Look who it is!"

We put our cards down on the table, one of us pulled up a chair, we moved apart slightly – "united we can all fit," that was our motto – and Darkness sat down with us. We ordered more beers.

"How long has it been?"

Decades, it turned out. We wanted to know where he'd been all that time. His right hand drew a broad curve, encompassing the ocean that was sleeping at our feet, lethargic like an old dog, and beyond it, the whole world and its darkest corners.

"Around. Around, a lot. Really a lot . . ."

Wherever he'd been, he hadn't stopped winning. He was wearing a shirt with a gecko print, white trousers and shoes in the finest leather. He had his head protected by a genuine panama, those hats that, despite the name, were made by hand in Ecuador, and sold for a small fortune at the best hat shops in Paris or New York. On his left wrist he sported a heavy gold watch, which he waved before our astonished eyes.

"Ah, how everything's changed. Only yesterday I was the poor kid. I didn't even have the money to buy a football. You guys remember? Now I own the ball. I own the ball, the football pitch and the players."

When we tried to find out what professional sphere he moved in, Darkness shrugged, evasive:

"Business. Import-export."

He had come back to the country, he explained, driven by a patri-otic longing to be a part of the great adventure of reconstruction. He spoke in a monologue about his longing for several minutes. One of us even dared to recall the tough times we'd been through in the "firm trench" of socialism, eating swordfish and rice, nicknamed the "FAPLA belt," or rice and rice, for months on end, while those who'd now returned to harvest the generous fruits of peace had been traveling the world on foreign passports. Darkness ran his tongue over his lips and there was an anxious silence.

"There is no suffering harsher than exile."

Then he asked us to deal the cards, and we played for the rest of the afternoon. We saw the sun disappearing into the sea. The water turning dark and choppier. We lost with admirable dignity. Finally Darkness put down his cards.

"It's good to come home," he murmured. He smiled, satisfied. "I was getting tired of winning on my own."

The Man with the Light

For Miguel Petchkovsky and Paula Tavares

NICOLAU ALICERCES PESHKOV had an enormous head, or maybe the rest of him was simply too shriveled for it, but in any case, it definitely looked as though it had been attached to someone else's body by mistake. His hair, what was left of it, was red and weedlike, his face covered in freckles. His unlikely name, his even more extraordinary physiognomy – all due to the travels through the Huambo highlands of a wandering Russian, his father, who in his alcoholic ravings boasted of having served as an officer in the cavalry of Nicholas II. Besides the name and the freckles, Nicolau Alicerces Peshkov had inherited his father's passion for cinema and his old projector. It was precisely that name, those freckles, and that projector, which is to say, his Russian heritage, that nearly landed him in front of a firing squad.

He had just spent two days and a night hiding in a crate of dried fish. He'd been woken with a start by the roar of gunshots. He didn't know where he was – that was always happening to him. He sat up in his bed and tried to remember, as the gunfire outside grew. He had arrived at dusk, pedaling his old bicycle, he'd rented a room in the boarding house run by a Portuguese man, he'd said goodbye to little James, who had family in the village, and gone to bed. It was a small room. The bed was iron, with a wooden board across the top covered with a sheet, which was clean but very worn. An enamel chamber pot. On the walls, somebody had painted a blue angel. A good picture. The angel looked straight at him, looked at something that wasn't there, with the same luminous and hopeless aloofness as Marlene Dietrich.

Nicolau Alicerces Peshkov, whom the Mucubal people called The Man with the Light, opened the window of his room, hoping to discover the reasons for the war. He peered out and saw that all along the road an armed mob was moving, some of them soldiers, mostly young civilians with little red ribbons tied round their heads. One of the young men pointed, shouting, and then another opened fire toward him. Nicolau still didn't know what war this was, but he understood that, regardless, he was on the wrong side of it. He left the bedroom in his underpants, went into the kitchen, opened a door and found a long and narrow back yard, blocked at the far end by a high adobe wall. He managed to jump the wall by climbing a rather squalid mango tree that grew alongside it, and found himself in another yard, this one broader, more abandoned, next to a wattle-and-daub hut that looked like it was used as a storeroom. He thought about James Dean. What would he do in this situation? James would definitely know what to do, he was an expert in getting away. He saw a laundry tank, filled up to the top with water, covered by a tarp. James Dean would get inside the tank, and he'd stay there, as long as he needed, waiting to grow scales. He, however, would not fit into that prison himself. Well, his body might, actually, but not his head. This was the state of despair he was in, hearing the mob getting closer, when he noticed the crate of fish. The smell was appalling, a strong stench of rotting seas, but it had just enough space for a crouching man. And so he climbed into the crate and waited.

Looking out through a gap in the crate, he saw the mob with the ribbons arrive. They were dragging five unfortunate guys by the neck, pushing them forward with kicks and blows from their rifle-butts, men whose only crime, it seemed, was speaking Umbundu. They laid them down on their backs and resumed their beating, with their weapons, with their belts, with heavy sticks, shouting that this was just for starters. A woman holding a pistol appeared, she moved the aggressors aside with a glance, held the gun to the neck of one of the poor wretches and fired. Then she did the same to the other four. Next, they brought over two young lads and four older women, one of them with a small child on her back, all of them crying and wailing. When they saw the bodies, the screaming increased. One of the soldiers cocked his gun: "Anybody who cries over the dead dies too."

The others started smacking the group around, not even sparing the child, while a guy with a video camera danced around them.

Nicolau Alicerces Peshkov moved his face away from the gap, and shut his eyes. It was no good: even with his eyes closed, he could see two of the young men rape one of the women; he saw them kill the child, with blows from their rifle butts, and the rest of the group with gunshots and kicks.

He emerged from the crate the next evening. He was so exhausted, and such was the torment in his puny breast, that he didn't notice the soldier sitting right beside the crate, watching over the corpses. The man looked at him with surprise, as happy as a little boy who'd just found the lucky charm in the fruitcake, and he led him by the hand to the police station. A very tall, thin man with a full beard was standing at the door when they arrived. He seemed to be waiting for them. They took him to a windowless room, made him sit on a chair. The tall man asked his name.

"Peshkov? Nicolau Peshkov?! You're Russian, comrade? That's very convenient – I studied in Moscow, at the Lubyanka, I speak Russian better than Portuguese."

And he unleashed a stream of impenetrable gibberish that

seemed to amuse everybody. Nicolau Peshkov laughed, too, seeing the others laugh, but only out of politeness, because what he really needed to do was cry.

The tall man turned abruptly serious. He pointed to a leather suitcase on his desk. "Do you know what this is?" Nicolau Peshkov recognized it as the case in which he kept his projector and his movies. He explained who he was. He had been travelling the country for forty years with that machine. He was proud of having brought the seventh art to the most remote and hidden corners of Angola – places forgotten by the rest of the world. In colonial times, he'd traveled by train. Benguela, Ganda, Chianga, Lépi, Catchiungo, Chinguar, Cutato, Catabola, Camacupa, Munhango, Luena. Wherever the train happened to stop, he would get out. He would unfurl the screen, position the projector on the tripod, set up half a dozen canvas chairs for the dignitaries of the town. People would come from far away, from the surrounding bush-country, from places with secret names, even some with no names at all. They would offer him goats, chickens, eggs, game meat. They would watch the movie from behind the screen, facing into the projector's light.

The war that followed independence destroyed the railroad and he was tied to the outskirts of the big cities. He soon lost everything he had managed to earn in the preceding twenty years. He concentrated on the south. He traveled by bicycle, with his assistant, the young James Dean, between Lubango and Humpata, between Huíla and Chibia. Sometimes he risked going down to Mossâmedes. Maybe Porto Alexandre. Baía dos Tigres. Never anywhere else. He would carry a white sheet, he would attach it to the wall of a hut, any wall would do, he'd set up the projector and run the movie. James Dean would pedal the whole time to produce the electricity. On a tranquil, moonless night, there was no cinema better.

The tall man listened to him with interest. He took some notes.

"And you can prove you really are the citizen you claim to be?"

Prove it? Nicolau Peshkov took a yellowing piece of paper from his shirt pocket and unfolded it carefully. It was a cutting from the *Jornal de Angola*. An interview published five years earlier: "The Last Cinema Hero." In the photo, which was black and white, Nicolau Alicerces Peshkov could be seen posing next to his bicycle, hands on the handlebars, his enormous head slightly out of focus.

The tall man snatched the cutting, turned it over and started to read some article or other about the importance of bombó flour. "It's not that one, boss," groaned Nicolau Peshkov, "please, just read the story on the other side. Look at the photo. That's me." The tall man looked at him with contempt:

"Comrade Peshkov, a man like you, who can't even speak his father's language, you'd tell me what I should and shouldn't read?!"

He read the article to the end. No, not right to the end, because it was cut off halfway.

"Where's the rest of this article?"

Nicolau Alicerces Peshkov spoke slowly.

"Please, boss . . . that's not the article. The relevant article, the one that means I can prove that I really am myself, that article is on the other side."

The tall man lost his patience.

"Fuck! You think we're all stupid here?! I'm asking where the rest of this article is. If you don't answer I'll have you shot for hiding information. I'm going to count to ten."

Maybe he doesn't know how to count to ten, thought Nicolau Peshkov. But unfortunately, he did. He counted to ten, slowly, and then turned his chair around and sat for a few long moments facing the wall. Then he turned around, opened the suitcase on his desk and took out the projector.

"Right, you little stooge – show us this movie, then. I want to see what it is you've been filming. Military targets, I'll bet."

Nicolau Peshkov asked for a clean sheet, a hammer and nails. He stretched out the sheet and nailed it to the wall. He set the projector up on a chair. He didn't say a word. He had learned a lot these past few hours. The movie was, in its way, his own work. The work of a lifetime. He had put it together, almost frame by frame, using what remained of his father's movies. He asked for the light to be turned out. One of the soldiers climbed onto a stool and carefully unscrewed the bulb from the ceiling.

Peshkov plugged the machine into the electricity and an utterly pure light fell onto the sheet. The first scene showed a family being attacked by birds inside their own home. This episode had a real impact on the viewers (it always did). The tall man spoke for all of them: "Did you see that?! Like wild dogs, those birdies are." Then they saw an old man perched on a roof playing a violin. "It's to drive away the birds," concluded one of the guards. "The guy's a sorcerer." There was also a cowboy kissing his girlfriend in front of a waterfall. Finally, a man with sad eyes, hat on his head, saying goodbye to a couple at an airport. When the couple boarded their plane, another guy appeared with a gun, but the one in the hat was quicker and shot him. Most likely the couple were running away from those birds. *The End.*

The projector light trembled, and went out, then there was a great silence. Finally, the tall man stood up, climbed onto the stool and screwed the ceiling bulb back in. He sighed.

"You can go, Peshkov. Get out of here. The movie stays."

Nicolau Alicerces Peshkov went out into the street. An enormous moon shone over the sea. He drew a comb from the back pocket of his trousers, and used it to smooth down what was left of his red hair.

Then he straightened up and went in search of James Dean. The kid would know what to do.

Flaming Flamingos, Flamboyants, and the Flemish

CARLOS DA MAIA was complaining about the flamingos. Damn flamingos. He disliked flamingos almost as much as he disliked the Flemish. Ega was surprised by his friend's aversion. They had seen, moments earlier, a pink cloud rising from the sea and floating across the sky. For Ega, that long moving flame had been reminiscent of a canvas by the Norwegian painter, Edvard Munch, which had annoyed countless critics. Doctors had advised pregnant women against looking at the picture.

"Those wise colleagues of mine were absolutely correct," pronounced Carlos, somberly. "I've seen that godforsaken canvas myself, too. I remember it well, very well, it's part of a group of six oil paintings. The last one Munch called *The Scream*, or *Despair*, isn't that right? Well, let me tell you, meaningless art like that is unquestionably harmful to pregnant women, and to the fetuses those poor wretches are carrying in their bellies."

Ega was horrified:

"You don't believe what you're saying, Carlos. Modern art . . ."

Carlos interrupted him:

"Modern art? Just that word 'modern' is enough to claw at my innards. Everything that's modern is harmful to us. The future is an inhospitable place. So much so that nobody lives there. As for those flamingos, every month I get five or six of the English coming to me shivering with fever. Paludism, João: the frightful malaria! The English like to go adventuring even to the mangroves, so as to see the flamingos better. They forget that the air around there is poisoned by malignant miasmas . . ."

"Really, Carlos – *miasmas*?"

"What's the problem with that? It's a good word. I like the old ones. But yes, the truth is that the mangroves are full of mosquitos. It's those mosquitos that transmit the disease." Carlos paused. He savored his cigar, while toying with the words. "Flaming flamingos and *flamboyants*. *Femmes fatales*. Fevers and inflammation. Everything flaming is attracted to this city."

João da Ega laughed.

"And the Flemish?"

Carlos gestured with his chin toward a group of five guys, beside one of the canopies, a hundred meters ahead. They all wore long beards, big, wide-brimmed hats, and they looked a little bored. Unlike the other spectators, who were watching the races with passion, cheering the horses on, these five bearded men were talking to one another, distractedly, as if they were the only people around.

"Those are my Flemish chaps. Well, Flemish from the Union of South Africa. Boers. They're responsible for the transportation of materials for the construction of the railway. They use carts pulled by teams of oxen. You've got to see it, one of these days, it's an astonishing sight. They use as many as thirty teams of oxen. They work well, they work hard, but they're coarse and intractable. Almost all of them are illiterate. Some of the ones you see there fought against the English. They talk some total shambles of a language, incomprehensible, it's not even Dutch anymore."

"All your dislike of these poor people, who you even admit are hard workers, it's to do with the fact they don't read *The Times* or *Le Figaro*? That they don't take care of their nails? They don't know how to choose a necktie? I'm quite sure it's not because they fought against the English . . ."

Carlos shook his head, smiling. The two friends, sitting in canvas chairs, beside a small canopy, differentiated themselves from the rest of the Europeans by being the only ones dressed in white. Seven employees were toiling away around them. Two were setting up a small table. A third was heating water on a fire. The others shook the air with large fans of ostrich feathers, in a useless attempt not only to cool the Portuguese gentlemen, but principally to shift the dust, which had been raised by the horses, and which had already tinged all the canopies with an even ochre color. All it would take would be for the wind to change direction, blowing a little harder, and that whole effort at civilization would be buried.

"The fact of their having fought the English makes them almost agreeable, and justifies my relative indulgence toward them," Carlos went on. "Consider, for example, the case of this firm. It will be, soon, and for many long years, the most important firm in our colonies. Yet it is not ours. It's English. How can we hand the development of Angola over to the English and still believe that Angola belongs to us?"

"It doesn't. Not Angola, nor Mozambique either."

"We have seven thousand Nigerians and Senegalese here, as well as two thousand Indians, who've come from Durban, contracted to lay the tracks, because, according to the English engineers, our people don't like working."

"Well, if we don't like it, why would they?"

"We don't like working. Neither us nor our blacks. We prefer pleasant conversation, around a nice stew, or, as we're doing now, savoring a fine red wine, smoking a good cigar, while we remain sitting down, watching the efforts of others."

"Those steeds, in this case . . ."

"Just so," Carlos agreed, drawing out a glow on his cigar. "Watching the efforts of the steeds."

"Has it never occurred to you that we might be right? The people of the north need to work, to sow in spring and harvest in autumn, otherwise what are they going to eat during the long, terrible winter months that await them each year? But us, or, even more so, these good people, the Angolans, the Brazilians, people blessed by nature with a perpetual summer, why should they need to work?"

"Maybe you're right."

"There's nothing wrong with idleness. The greatest criminals in the history of humanity, those of the past, those of this foul present, and all those that are to come, they all have one characteristic in common: hyperactivity. The lazy ones, meanwhile, only ever dare the tiniest of crimes. Hatred demands energy. Grandiose hatred demands enormous energy. To kill somebody you've got to be standing up. Whereas loving – that's best done lying down."

"More comfortably, in any event . . ."

"You see, evil's not to be found in idleness. What's evil is suffering idleness as though it were a sin. And who instilled this error in us? The priests, my dear Carlos, the Church. The biggest difference between our colonies and the English colonies has got to do with the rigor of faith. The Calvinists, like those five disagreeable Flemish fellows of yours, are very much more intolerant than the Catholics, first and foremost because they pray only to one single god."

"And don't Catholics pray to the same god?"

"Come now, Carlos, who do you think my blessed mother prayed to, who did she turn to, desperate, whenever she saw me arriving home drunk, squandering the inheritance that papá had left us, not on books, not on visits to the opera or journeys to Paris and the Holy Land, but on the purest debauchery?"

"I imagine she prayed to the Virgin . . ."

"Well there you have it. She prayed to the Virgin. She didn't pray to the one single god, abstract and infinitely tedious, the Calvinists' one. She prayed to the Virgin! And who is this Virgin, breast-feeding the baby Jesus, if not Isis breast-feeding Horus? And now tell me, who does my devout sister pray to when it thunders?"

"To Santa Barbara, of course. And you don't need to add more saints, now I see where you're going. In your opinion, Catholicism is an embarrassed pantheism whose divinities have been stolen from other religions. Am I right? But does that make the Catholics any more tolerant?"

"No doubt about it. Whoever believes in a single god, believes in a single truth, that is to say, they are a fanatic. Whoever worships many divinities tends to cohabit with others' truths more easily. Just look at how, in Brazil, Christianity got mixed up with the barbarian superstitions of the slaves."

"Could be. But what's that got to do with what we were talking about before, the Portuguese dislike of work?"

"It's got everything to do with it. As I was telling you, idleness isn't what's evil. What's evil is believing idleness a terrible evil. We Catholics believe that, we're taught to believe that, though without the degree of guilt and terror the Calvinists have. The Calvinists, including those from the Union of South Africa, are so appalled by idleness that they even work. They work hard. We just have the guilt."

"Your project, then, your project in life, your great ambition, your entire philosophy, is putting an end to this pernicious feeling of guilt . . ."

"Exactly. Laziness without guilt, that's my motto."

Carlos drew on his cigar one last time, put it down in the ashtray, and rose after a protracted sigh. The races were coming to an end. Gentlemen were jostling one another toward the finishing post. Occasionally one of them, one of the luckier, the more euphoric ones, would toss his top hat into the air. One of these top hats flew over the canopy of the two Portuguese gentlemen, like a crazy bird, before disappearing round the back, swallowed up by the dust.

"We lost," said Carlos, sadly. "Our horse lost. Definitely a Catholic."

"Definitely," said João da Ega, trying to straighten up. "My whole body is disjointed and aching. First it was the trip on the steamer, days and days stretched out in the sun, looking out at the same sea, then your race, the heat, the humidity, the dust. I'm sweating, all crumpled up, absolutely worn out. Would you take me to the hotel?"

Scene Two – The Hunt

João da Ega stopped, breathless, in the lacy shadow of a large acacia. He leaned his rifle, which was weighing heavily in his hands, against the wrinkled trunk of the tree, and pulled the colonial helmet off his head. Then, slowly, he unfolded a huge yellow handkerchief and ran it across his smooth skull, his face, his neck, wiping away the sweat. He had never walked so much. The landscape ahead of him was crackling with whiteness and with heat. He wouldn't have been surprised if, all of a sudden, the whole thing had exploded into roaring flames. Carlos, who was a few meters ahead, turned around, looking at him with a mocking smile. On his head was a light panama and he was as cool, as well rested, as if he had woken up only moments earlier, not there, not in that radiant and sticky hell, but in some tidy, balmy spring, in Switzerland or Brittany.

"Well, my dear old *John*, your legs are already weighing you down?"

The other man grunted, annoyed. He had been moved to accept his friend's challenge by curiosity, and by the pleasure of imagining himself, five weeks later, having a few beers with the lads, back at one of the tables at the Brasileira Café or the Hotel Central. He foresaw, with happy pleasure, the expression, a mixture of astonishment and envy, on the face of fat Dâmaso or young Diamantino Cunha, his colleague at the Court of Auditors, when he told them, with feigned indifference, how he'd brought down a forest buffalo – or a lion, why the hell not a lion?! – with a perfect shot. In the end they hadn't spotted any forest buffalos, or any lions, just a rabbit, a runty little rabbit, against which he had gotten himself all worked up with heavy rifle shots, and which, finally, one of Carlos's three gundogs had brought down with its teeth.

"Don't lose heart, child!" Carlos was laughing. "Give Domingos the rifle. Drink your water and rouse your legs. There's only two more hours and you'll see the surprise will be worth it."

João da Ega handed the rifle to the tracker, who was already carrying one, along with the rabbit, and they resumed their walking. They were accompanied by a son of the land, the journalist Benjamim

Viçoso – a portly, energetic fellow, with powerful hands and a lovely bass voice – and a very red-headed American missionary, Robert Heywood, who had only arrived in Benguela five years earlier but already spoke Portuguese and Umbundu with extraordinary fluency.

"The hunt isn't the important thing," Carlos had said when inviting his friend. And then he'd added, mysteriously: "I want to show you a marvel!" João da Ega presumed this was going to be some miracle of nature – a vast baobab, even bigger, and wider, than the ones that had surprised him in the outskirts of the city, perhaps some geological curiosity or other. Or maybe the antelope with gigantic horns that a Belgian engineer, Henry Frank Varian, who was similarly in the service of the railway, had discovered a few years earlier.

He had never imagined this.

In the distance, floating over the limpid light of the horizon, he first saw the slow fluttering of wings. He realized, as they approached, that they were not in fact wings but sails. Torn, loose sails fluttering in the warm evening breeze. The boat asserted itself gradually, like a dream taking possession of reality. It was a small, two-masted schooner, with the most beautiful outline, buried amid the tall grass. On the flank, it was possible to make out the drawing of a mulatta mermaid, lying on her side, covering one of her breasts demurely with her left hand, while her right held a board on which the name of the craft could be read: "Dream." Ega stroked the sun-cracked paint, perplexed:

"How many kilometers from the sea are we?!"

Carlos smiled, happy at his friend's amazement.

"About fifteen. Maybe more."

"So how the devil did this end up here?!"

Benjamim Viçoso was expecting the question. He sat down on the sand, in the redemptive shade of the craft.

"Not everyone knows the story. It's a good story." He pulled out a small metal canteen, took out the stopper, and held it out to João da Ega. "Have a bit to drink. You needn't worry, it's not water. I don't drink water."

Ega had a gulp and spat it out to the side, quite distressed. The Angolan laughed, a laugh that was big and without malice:

"Sit down, João. Sit next to me. I can see you need to rest a bit. I'll tell you how this boat ended up here."

It was his father who'd shown him the boat, and explained to him how it had come to be there. Around 1830, a sailor disembarked in Luanda, exiled to Angola for committing a murder. He had left his name behind, along with his past, so he was given a new one: N'Zoji. Apparently N'Zoji had killed another sailor in a brawl. In Luanda, he started out by working in a tavern. As soon as he was able to accumulate some capital, he bought fabrics and wines and set off for the interior. He set up a store in the outskirts of Dombe Grande, and in ten years, through trading bad wine for passable palm oil, good rubber and excellent ivory, he had become a rich man. In the meantime he had shacked up with the daughter of a local chief, a man famous across the region as a healer. They had twelve children. One day, a caravan came past. N'Zoji was watching uninterested as the banners and drums paraded past, the racket of the bearers, the sad slave dirges, when all of a sudden he felt as though he was awaking from a dream. Stretched out on a litter, surrounded by happy urchins, there followed a mulatta girl, with long wavy hair loose over her shoulders. N'Zoji smiled at her, she returned the smile and he thought that the delicate brilliance coming from her perfect lips was the most beautiful spectacle in the world.

Blind with passion, the trader decided to quit his family, his home and his business, and follow the young woman to Luanda. It seemed nothing could talk him out of it. At that point, his wife, in a state of desperation, asked her father for help. The old healer – momentarily inspired – cast an odd spell on the Portuguese man. No sooner did N'Zoji try to move more than two hundred meters from the family home than the poor man struggled to breathe and fell to the ground, writhing and gasping like a fish out of water. Thus hindered from leaving, the former sailor started to dream about the sea. In the rainy season, as he started to watch the light undulation of the green grass, he felt an insuppressible nostalgia for those long days he had spent sailing the waters. In the dry season, the acacias, from a distance, reminded him of ships lost in the mist.

He had carpenters brought from Luanda to build a schooner. The project took him a whole year. There was a river, nameless, forgotten, that flowed gently, skirting the house, and the fields of corn and cassava right behind it. N'Zoji ordered that a dam be built, thus creating a small lagoon. Like this he was able to go sailing, or have the impression that he was sailing, within two hundred short meters, for the remaining eighteen years of his life. His wife survived him by only a dozen days. His children gave up the shop and scattered across the country. The lagoon dried up.

Benjamim Viçoso fell silent. He had another slug of cachaça, took a deep breath, reinvigorated, and offered the canteen to João da Ega. The Portuguese man declined. Carlos sat down beside him.

"I don't know what you make of that story, João, and I'd rather not know. I'm getting old, and as I get old I think I'm getting more prone to dreaming. These last few years I've become practically romantic. Your skepticism, which used to entertain me, terrifies me now. Honestly, what is the matter with you? Personally, I find it a lovely parable. It does occur to me occasionally that this enchantment, the spell cast on the sailor by the old chief, is something more current in this country than one might suppose. How else might one explain how so many foreigners, who come to visit Angola, end up staying here for the rest of their lives? Yes, they have to face that sum total of discomforts that you've complained about so much, the heat, the humidity, the mosquitos, the malaria, the impossibility of reading *The Times* except with a one-month delay, the fact of there not being a decent place for drinking tea or getting your beard trimmed, etc. etc. And yet they stay, they never go back to the comfort of their homes. They have trouble catching their breath the moment they step away from this red ground. I don't know whether I'll ever see Chiado again myself . . ."

"Ai, what an appalling thing to say, Carlos!" wailed João da Ega. And he was saying it with genuine abhorrence. "I know that Lisbon didn't treat you well. But beyond Portugal, there's the whole of civilized Europe. You could have stayed in Paris, or gone to London, to Rome, cities where you'd be sheltered from spiteful gossip but where a man like you has the possibility of a dignified way of life."

Benjamim Viçoso, who had been following the Portuguese men's conversation, now amused, now irritated, sprang up, moving like a dancer, with a surprising elasticity and elegance in one so portly, and launched into a passionate defense of Angola, and of Benguela in particular. The Angolans had suffered greatly, over the centuries, he bellowed, due to the neglect with which the metropolis treated the colony. Truth be told, Portugal only wanted quick plunder, the gold, the slaves, and more recently the coffee or cocoa, they didn't much care about the territory's progress or that of its wretched inhabitants. Until the end of the slave trade, there was a greater, more robust link to Rio de Janeiro than to Lisbon. In spite of this neglect, he added, the Angolans had managed to create a robust press. In these newspapers, poets and thinkers had been revealed. The country was vast, rich, generous. "The day will come," he prophesied, pointing his finger, "when Portugal will kneel before a free and independent Angola to beg for a hunk of bread." João da Ega was listening to him, amazed.

"That may well happen," he sighed. "Kneeling is an exercise we are very good at. There cannot be many countries in the world that kneel with such pleasure and such skill as we."

SCENE THREE – DOMESTIC LIFE

The woman undid her dressing gown. A constellation of small coppery moles tumbled down her neck, over her shoulders, over her breasts, like confetti scattered over her on a carnival night. When he had first had her in his arms, so many years ago, her skin was smooth, clean and so glowing that she seemed able to light up even the most forlorn of nights. That was a long time ago now, that was yesterday. Carlos felt he was falling, as if the ground had been taken from him, and shut his eyes. Maria Eduarda was concerned:

"What's wrong?"

The man smiled. He held his arms out to her, and she came to nestle in them. It was nothing, he reassured her. It pained him, sometimes, the passing of time. He had fallen asleep on his grandfather's lap and when he woke up the old man was dead, and he had lost the family home, his strength and the dreams of his youth. Time steals everything from us. The woman stroked his thinning hair. She stroked his face. She kissed his lips, a light touch at first, then furiously, urgently. Her fingers moved down his shoulders, down his chest, through the gray hair.

"You don't regret it?"

Carlos didn't regret it.

"Love is never wrong."

He had been saying that for years. Of course love can be wrong, indeed it happens with some frequency. Carlos knew this. He would say those words, not to convince himself, nor even in an attempt to convince Maria, but merely to hide with this false reply the lack of any better one. He didn't regret having gone to meet her, in Paris, after the death of his grandfather, old Afonso da Maia. He had bought a small mansion, in the Place des Vosges, and had settled there, with her and with little Rosa.

On a brief visit to Lisbon, years later, he had told his friends, João da Ega among them, that Maria was set to marry some "*gentilhomme campagnard*, from a serious family, with a fortune." Nobody found the weak lie surprising. Nobody demolished him with questions. Men's memory is fleeting and elusive, and besides, life in the meantime had spun tastier scandals than this. Carlos and Maria traveled around various countries. On one occasion, in Bayreuth, as they were leaving the opera, they saw – terrified! – a fellow raising his walking stick and coming toward them, breaking through all the appalled Germanic composure with a barbaric southern shout:

"Carlos!"

It was Cruges, old Cruges, with the curly hair, gray now, cascading down over his sharp shoulder bones.

"Carlos! How lovely to see you! Nothing like seeing Parsifal in the very place where it was born, eh?!"

He was so enraptured that he went on talking for another five minutes about Wagner, about the unique conditions of the Festspielhaus, about redemption through love. Only then, as he was catching his breath, did he seem to notice Maria. Carlos spoke:

"You two already know each other, I think? . . ."

Cruges said yes right away, kissing Maria's hand. He obviously had no idea who this woman was. They said goodbye with a promise to have dinner, the following day, in a little restaurant of a friend of Cruges' at which, the pianist assured them, they prepared some quite decent partridges, and where they wouldn't run the risk of having to face another dish of sauerkraut or those stubborn Bavarian sausages. The following day, in the morning, Carlos and Maria left for Berlin.

The two lovers' main concern was always Rosa, the daughter Maria had had, years earlier, from a very brief liaison with a young Irishman who had been killed fighting the Germans in the battle of Saint-Privat. They were unsure what to do. They could tell her the truth – "Carlos is your uncle!" – and hide the affair. Or they could acknowledge the relationship, traveling the world as a legitimate couple, but hiding the horror of the incest from her. Finally, they decided it would be best to conceal the affair in front of the girl, of the household staff and of all those relationships that, in the meantime, they would come to develop. Maria would be the widow, with a young daughter, whom her bachelor brother had chosen to take in. For years the arrangement worked out. It may be that the servants thought the displays of affection between sister and brother a little over the top, but none of them ever made the least comment. Rosa studied in a convent school in Orléans, spending two or three months a year with her mother and uncle. At sixteen, she was already an exceptionally beautiful woman, tall and elegant, with long hair, quite perfectly blond, like a more Nordic and more refined version of Maria. She had a voice identical to her mother's, which allowed her to play tricks on her uncle. One such joke ended in great misfortune.

By this time, Rosa was starting to study medicine, at the Université de Montpellier, one of the oldest in the world. Maria had been against her daughter's intentions, believing them sheer folly, but Carlos supported his niece. He saw in her enthusiasm some of his own when, at that same age, he had left for Coimbra. He was pleased, too, at the courage she showed, confronting a society for whom a woman's place was in the smothering of the home, taking care of her husband and looking after the children. In this young woman he sensed a determination he had never had. Passion, yes, Carlos had experienced bursts of passion, sudden raptures – for some project or other, for some particular writer or artist, for a woman – but he would quickly tire.

In the second week of the new century, Carlos traveled by train from Paris to Lisbon, in an effort to resolve some problems related to the administering of a number of properties. Ever since old Vilhaça's death, it had been one of his sons, fat Diogo, who had managed the Maias' inheritance. Unfortunately, the aforementioned inheritance had drained away, year after year, like sand in an hourglass. One rough evening, struggling with heaps of paper laden with inauspicious numbers, Carlos returned to the Hotel Central, where he had settled, feeling old and tired. After a long bath, with his soul washed pure and serene, he decided to phone Maria. He had had a telephone installed, some months earlier, in the mansion in the Place des Vosges. The servants didn't go anywhere near the instrument, terrified by those disembodied voices that traveled along thin copper wires. He asked the operator to call Paris. After a few brief seconds he heard another woman's voice, in gentle French, whom he informed of the telephone number. A few more moments' wait, a metallic crackling, then he recognized the gentle voice of his lover.

Carlos was happy to hear her. He was overtaken by a sudden tenderness for that woman who knew him so well and who forgave the mistakes and frailties of his soul. A woman who had gone on loving him, even while knowing that their love was both a crime and a sin.

"I miss you," he murmured. "It's good to hear your voice."

"Me too, love. I was thinking about you."

That was how the Admiral seized possession of him. Ah, yes – we must introduce the Admiral. Carlos disapproved of (while at the same time enjoying) certain of João da Ega's verbal excesses, the scathing or risqué quips with which the former Law student shocked friends and strangers. Ega sought to excuse himself:

"It's not me who's saying those outrageous things. It's as if there were some devil speaking through me."

The two men came to refer to this alleged devil, jokingly, as the Admiral. This being might descend at any moment, though he preferred to do so in the presence of beautiful young women. From a certain point, perhaps through some contagion, Carlos began likewise to be affected by him. In the brief visit he had paid to Lisbon, ten years after running away to Paris, it had made one of these appearances. It was a sleepy Sunday in August and Carlos was walking down through Chiado, in the company of João da Ega. They were casually discussing what was wrong with the world, when they saw a tall, languid woman getting out of a blue caleche, with a turbulent head of hair of a black so deep that, for a few moments, the afternoon light faltered, swallowed up by it. This was Rachel Cohen, wife of Jacob Cohen, esteemed director of the National Bank. She was with a small, coquettish woman, whom Rachel introduced to the two men with a nervous smile, as being a German friend. João da Ega had, years earlier, maintained an ardent romance with Rachel. This affair was discovered by her husband. There was no great tragedy. Jacob threw João out of his house, and then thrashed Rachel with his walking stick. It was a redemptive experience for them both. From that night on, Jacob's walking stick, rattan topped with a greyhound head, became the symbol of a perverse erotic game which, as the years went by, the couple only continued to perfect. Jacob began to punish his wife, devotedly, passionately, with a fierce joy – agreeing, occasionally, to have the roles reversed – and in this cheerful way succeeded in rescuing a previously disastrous marriage. The conjugal happiness had positively rejuvenated Rachel. Carlos, who hadn't seen her in a decade, was struck by the change:

"Has milady done a deal with the Devil?! You're looking younger, cooler, even more beautiful . . ."

The gallantry was received with a slow batting of eyelashes, a modest smile:

"Thank you. I think I married the Devil."

"I can believe it," said Carlos, or said the Admiral through his lips. "Jacob certainly does have much of the Devil in him. At least, to judge by those horns . . ."

João da Ega launched himself onto his friend, annoyed, the moment the two women had vanished:

"What has got into you, damn it?"

Carlos gave his shoulders a shake, as if by doing this he might be able to shake the whole ignoble moment out of his life:

"I swear it wasn't me, child. It was the Admiral."

That winter afternoon, at the Hotel Central, it was also the Admiral who whispered those vulgar words into the mouthpiece, which Maria might even have found amusing, if she had been on the other end. However, the person on the other end was Rosa. There was a moment of icy silence. Then the sound of a voice, almost in tears:

"Uncle?! I don't understand . . ."

Then the line went dead. Carlos sat down on the floor, drained of all strength, frozen with dread. He got up with some effort and asked the operator to reconnect the call. Nobody answered. It was night by the time he managed to speak to his sister. He found her having a breakdown. She was crying. Shouting hysterical fragments of phrases that Carlos struggled to understand:

"Was it you? What did you do? What did you do to my little girl? . . ."

Carlos returned to France the following day. He found, on his arrival, the house plunged into an atmosphere of mourning. The servants murmured to one another, eyes lowered, beneath the bitter shadows. Maria was locked in her room. She only allowed him to come in after countless entreaties. She told him that Rosa had arrived, without warning, to spend a few days at home. She'd seemed happy with her studies. Then, suddenly, after receiving a phone call from Carlos, she showed up in the library, very upset, clutching a suitcase and saying she was leaving and not to try to stop her. She threw her mother a note and left. Maria showed it to her brother:

"For years I've refused to see what was right under my nose. I don't

know what to think. *I'm dying of shame. Don't look for me. I want to start again with a new life, somewhere far away, very far away, from this utter horror.*"

Maria allowed herself to slip into a deep depression. What happened with Carlos was the opposite: the tragedy woke him up. He committed himself, on the one hand, to recovering Maria's trust and love, and, on the other, to finding Rosa. He paid detectives to track her down. He followed up some clues himself. Seven months later, he found his niece in Amsterdam, living, very impoverished, in the studio of a young artist, Theorodus van den Hove, whose most significant glory was having spent a few days with the great French photographer Félix Nadar. The young man (younger even than Rosa) signed his canvases with the simple, and yet excessive, diminutive, Theo, thus confirming that in simplicity the most exalted arrogance can be hidden (or not, perhaps it was merely a diminutive). When she saw her uncle come in, Rosa shut herself in one of the bedrooms, and refused to talk to him. Carlos got annoyed. He shouted at the girl, while slapping furiously on the door. Theo interceded:

"I beg you, sir, please, do leave . . ."

Carlos left. That same day he hired a *marchand* to start buying Theo's canvases, which, over the years, he accumulated in one of the bedrooms of the mansion in the Places des Vosges. He even went so far as to pay an art critic to publish, in a Parisian newspaper, half a dozen pieces of praise to the Flemish boy's art. He wrote to Rosa many times. He never received a reply.

In 1906, Carlos read a lengthy article in an English newspaper about the building of a railroad in Angola, which was set to cross the whole territory, from Benguela to the Belgian border at Katanga. The grandeur of the project excited him. He fell asleep, and in his dream he saw the workers opening up a trail of light through the slow African savannahs. He offered himself up as a doctor to the company staff. The move helped Maria, who in recent years, since Rosa's flight, had done nothing but tend to her own melancholy. The company provided them with a lovely mansion, built of wood, in the colonial style, in the Restinga do Lobito neighborhood. Maria filled it with flowers and songs.

Carlos, stretched out in bed, watching over his lover's sleep, was thinking about everything that had happened to them in the last few years. No, no, he didn't regret it. Through the window there came a light that was soft and colored, like palm oil, along with the cool commotion of the waves, the vague barking of a dog in some distant yard. Carlos got up, put on a dressing gown, and went out onto the veranda. The sea climbed the beach, and swept over the wooden boards, bathing his bare feet. The enormous moon, very round, very red, hanging on the highest branches of a casuarina, looked like a curious fruit, just ready to drop.

He heard a car engine. He walked around the veranda and saw, in the distance, on the road, the uncertain light of a pair of headlamps. A Model T Ford stopped outside the house. The driver got out, removed a suitcase, and then walked around the car and opened the other door. Carlos knew who she was even before he saw her face, the ample hair, quite perfectly blond, illuminated by the soft light of the moon.

The Interpreter of Birds

E MANUEL DIVINO TCHIMBAMBA learned to chirp during the years of the Angolan civil war. It was common practice among the guerrilla forces, to fool the government troops. The small groups of commandos communicated with one another, hidden in the tall grasses, by imitating the songs of the birds. Using codes, they would exchange important information: the number of enemy soldiers, what weapons they were carrying, which way they were headed, etc., etc., and so forth, or, as they say in Luanda, *kapuete kamundanda kapolokosso*.

Tchimbamba took the studying of chirping so seriously that he was able not only to deceive the government troops, but the birds themselves. He became famous for hunting partridges without firing a single shot, he'd merely call to them by their respective names. It was also said (but this might be merely a legend) that he commanded a squadron of falcons, eagles and hawks, which would fly over the enemy forces and then return, bringing him information.

When the war was over, Tchimbamba started to hire himself out. He was never short of work. The farmers would pay him to wander through the cornfields, imitating the cries of the hawks to scare off sparrows and other small birds. There were also men who hired him to organize recitals, on Sundays, very early in the morning, beneath the windows of the women they loved. Tchimbamba was able, on his own, to be an orchestra of birds. Sometimes, however, when he was not enjoying his solitude, he would call on other genuine birds to accompany him.

I interviewed Emanuel Divino Tchimbamba a few years back, in a huge market, now vanished, in the Angolan capital. The former guerrilla fighter had set up a little stall in the heart of that impeccable chaos, where he would receive anyone who might be interested in talking to an old owl, who Tchimbamba claimed was the spirit of the legendary chief Caparandanda. The owl, or Caparandanda through it, answered all sorts of questions, from the most domestic and trivial to the most complex and uncommon, with Tchimbamba acting as translator. Most of those consulting just wanted to know how much time they had left in their lives, whether their husbands had a lover, whether their clubs were going to win the national championships, *kapuete kamundanda kapolokosso*. There were, however, those who brought more difficult questions:

"Why do we die?"

"What is the point of pain?"

"What is time?"

Caparandanda would answer every question. These answers would often come in the form of proverbs, which Tchimbamba had some trouble translating, and whose interpretation would, in the weeks that followed, spawn endless debates over the family lunches of the unhappy inquirers.

I decided to try my luck. I sat down, looked the owl straight in the abyssal eye and asked:

"Will I ever be happy in love?"

The owl gave a series of quick, gloomy hoots, shut his eyes and fell silent.

"He's laughing," Tchimbamba translated.

Well, that was just a total lack of respect, I thought. Nevertheless, it was an answer suited to the character of Caparandanda, a chief who terrorized the Portuguese traders at the end of the nineteenth century, attacking the caravans that transported ivory and rubber, and distributing their plunder around the local populations. I thought for a moment:

"Will we ever stop having wars in the world?"

I wanted to hear him laugh again. That didn't happen. The owl wailed a long reply, which with some effort Tchimbamba translated:

"He's saying that in the same way men have skin covering their bodies, they have shadow covering their hearts. He's saying that to eat an ant's liver you must first learn to disembowel it."

I left convinced that Tchimbamba was an agreeable, imaginative swindler. I recently learned the news of his death. The people who informed me were unable to tell me the cause. He was with a group of friends, just chatting, he felt unwell, asked for a glass of water, and died. Simple as that. As he himself used to say, death is a job for the poor.

I thought about the owl's words again, or Caparandanda's, or Tchimbamba's, it makes no difference. Maybe they didn't mean anything. It's possible that, not knowing what to say, the old guerrilla simply had a bit of fun inventing obscure proverbs. I do think it an excellent strategy. Alternatively, from his perch on the highest branch of the tree of spirits, Caparandanda really could see the future, and he did not like what he saw.

The Tree that Swallowed Time

I HAVE A friend, the photographer Sérgio Guerra, who collects baobabs. When he first touched down in Luanda, coming from Salvador, nearly two decades ago, Sérgio was fascinated by the strange beauty of those rare baobabs that still survived in the Angolan capital's outer districts. One day he saw a group of local people getting ready to cut down one particularly huge specimen. He stopped his car and, talking to the workmen, he learned that the plot of land had been sold for somebody to build a house on. He went to see the owner and bought the land. The baobab is still there, recovering from a huge slash through its trunk, big enough for a man to lie down inside it. After this, many people sought out my friend, wanting to know whether he might be interested in buying plots of land with baobabs on them – threatening to cut down the baobabs if he didn't buy the land. He ended up buying several more.

I was at Sérgio's house, one morning in the dry season, when a thin, nervous-looking guy showed up, looking for the man who collected baobabs. Sérgio interrupted him, a little irritated, to inform him that, no, he was no longer in the baobab-buying business.

"It's not a baobab," said the man. "It's a very big mulemba tree and it's bewitched."

Sérgio had never been interested in mulembas (*Ficus thonningii*), even though they were incredibly beautiful trees, perhaps because there are species in Brazil that are very like it. The magical part, however, did catch his attention.

"What do you mean, bewitched?"

The man begged us to go with him. It was important that we see the marvel for ourselves. It had taken him some time to find Sérgio's house. He'd had to take two minibuses and walk a lot. If we went by car, however, it wouldn't take us more than half an hour. So off we went.

An hour and a half later we arrived at a narrow, beaten-earth lane, outside the city limits now. Behind a high wall spread the green branches of a huge mulemba. Somebody opened the gate and in we went.

There were a dozen men gathered around the mulemba's thick, intricate trunk. The air was dense with frozen bewilderment. One of the men, himself almost as fat as the mulemba, and with a head of hair that was just as thick and round, broke away from the others and came toward us:

"Gentlemen! You got to see this!"

The others moved aside, and we saw the harsh blows that had split the thick roots that hung from the vast tree. The blade of one of the axes had broken when it struck something hard. From out of the confusion of roots, a part of some solid shape was emerging, something iron, nearly twenty centimeters wide and thirty high.

"Amazing!" said Sérgio. "It's a safe!"

I remembered having seen photos of assorted iron objects found inside trees, or partly consumed by them: coins, bicycles, road signs and even war materiel. If you put an iron chain around a thick trunk, the trunk will end up absorbing the chain. Imagine somebody taking photos of the tree devouring the chain, at the same time every day, for years and years. Finally, by combining the pictures, we would see the tree devouring the chain in just a few minutes: a horror movie. That's what tree time is. They look at us and see little animals dashing about very quickly back and forth, getting older and then dying. To a mulemba, man is an ephemeral insect.

The countryfolk listened to me with their heads bowed, in an attentive silence that I naïvely took for respect. Then, the one who looked like a mulemba tutted quickly and concluded that the piece of land was bewitched. Sérgio smiled:

"Very well. How much do you want for it?"

Ten minutes later, they agreed on a price. That afternoon, Sérgio

143

Guerra became the happy owner of a useless bit of land and an enchanted mulemba tree. We returned home a little dazed.

"What are you going to do with the mulemba?" I asked.

Sérgio lit a cigarette. He sat back in his chair, watching the languid spirals of smoke disappearing into the air, and sighed:

"What do you think's inside that safe?"

"Treasure, or a curse, or a recipe for banana cake, or the love letters of an old Portuguese colonial?"

"I'll get somebody to open the safe tomorrow."

The following morning we returned to that piece of land, accompanied by Aristóteles Vapir, a former guerilla, who had worked for Sérgio for years as a driver, mechanic and able electrician. Aristóteles studied the tree, rapped on the side of the safe three times with his knuckles, and finally declared:

"You can cut into it with a blowtorch. Easy."

He went to the car to fetch the blowtorch. Sérgio sat down on a stone, in the shade of the mulemba, to roll a cigarette, and by the time Aristóteles had returned he'd already changed his mind:

"We're going to leave the safe as it is."

"You don't want to know what's inside?"

"A mystery – that's what's inside. As long as we don't open the safe, we'll always have a fine mystery. If we open it, I don't know what we'll have. Most likely nothing that interesting."

Whenever I go to Luanda, my friend takes me to pay a visit to the mulemba. If you push the branches aside, you can still see the safe. I put the palm of my hand onto the metal and feel the mystery pulsing within.

On the Perils of Laughter

IT WASN'T until we stopped the jeep that I saw them. There they were, on the side of the road, half hidden by the roar of dusk – the old man and his lizards. They were huge lizards and they had wrinkled necks just like the old man's and the same mysterious little eyes. He noticed my interest, and gave their price.

"Five million, buddy. Each one."

The price seemed fair, but it was worth haggling.

"Five million?! For five million they'd have to talk . . ."

The old man looked at me, very serious:

"Well, they do talk but not very much, man, it's true. But they do laugh a lot."

They laugh, the lizards?! At what? The old man shrugged. He didn't know. They laughed randomly, like lunatics, they laughed at one another while they sunned themselves. That answer alone, I thought, was enough to earn the old man his money. I gave him five bills, which he smoothed down carefully before tucking them away in his pocket. Then he handed me the largest of the lizards.

"His name's Leopoldino, this one, he's the very smartest."

I wanted to know what he ate. The old man explained that the creature could look after himself. He ate flies, cockroaches, mosquitoes, he kept the house free from insects. I tried to make a joke:

"And on top of that we can tell him jokes, right?"

The old man didn't answer. He leaned over the lizards and said something to them. He seemed to be speaking a language brought over from another world. He was speaking a breeze, a breath, a damp little vegetable murmur. I got into the jeep and watched him disappear, a shadow within the dark night, feeling somehow that he had made a fool of me.

However, as we were getting close to Sumbe, the lizard started to laugh. I know that's going to seem strange, but it's the absolute truth: Leopoldino was laughing. He wasn't laughing exactly like a person, of course, he was laughing like a person who resembled a lizard, but he was laughing. They were dry, cynical bursts of laughter that exploded into the jeep in a way that was faintly alarming. I heard him and I did not want to laugh. My friend, who was driving, was even more uneasy:

"What's that damn animal laughing at?"

I shrugged (as the old man had done). How was I supposed to

know? Maybe he was laughing randomly, like a lunatic. I told him that lizards of that species communicate with one another by laughing while they sun themselves. My friend, however, had a different opinion:

"No!" he said, "it's obviously laughing at us!"

That assumption implanted mistrust inside the jeep. I opened the shoebox where Leopoldino was being kept and put him in front of us on the dashboard. His eyes were ancient. Everything about him was ancient. The three of us watched one another in silence. The look in Leopoldino's eyes was challenging, perhaps a little arrogant, but I couldn't find in those eyes the slightest flicker of irony.

I tried to calm my friend.

"Parrots laugh, they even talk, but their laughter, and the stuff they say, it doesn't mean a thing. Well, reptiles are related to birds, so why shouldn't there be some reptiles that can imitate human laughter?"

My friend was starting to get nervous:

"Don't fuck with me! I know perfectly well when I'm being laughed at by a lizard . . ."

Well, put like that, the matter was personal now. A laugh can often be the worst kind of insult. On top of that, Leopoldino's laugh left the field wide open for any kind of speculation: he might be laughing at our ugliness (to reptiles we humans must be extremely ugly); he might be laughing at the stupidity of two guys buying a lizard for five million Kwanzas on the Luanda-Sumbe road; or maybe he knows something (about us) that it would be better for no one to know (not even our consciences). I said this just to make conversation, but my poor friend took what I'd said seriously:

"Must be because of that thing with Ana," he murmured grimly. "Damn creature knows stuff it shouldn't."

I didn't know what had happened between him and Ana; I didn't even know who Ana was, but I thought it best to keep my mouth shut. It must have been something spectacularly ridiculous. If he told me, I might not have been able to control my own laughter. And if I'd laughed myself at that point, our friendship would have been over.

"I haven't told you the worst part," I admitted. "If the old man's to be believed, he can also talk."

"He talks, the animal talks?! No, that's too much! . . ."

He pulled the jeep over to the side of the road, keeping the head-lights on, and jumped out onto the asphalt. In his right hand he was holding a pistol.

"I'm going to execute this guy!"

It was the first time I'd seen him armed. I leaped out of the jeep.

"Of course you aren't. The lizard's mine."

He looked at me and I realized he wasn't kidding. My friend had been through the war. Two years at Cuito Cuanavale.

"The lizard's mine," I said again. "Let me deal with this."

I took the gun from his hand, picked up the shoebox that had Leopoldino in it and moved a few meters away into the bush. The jeep's headlamps lit up the dry grass, the tall cacti, the broad outline of a baobab. In the vast, limpid, starry night, the only sound to be heard was the hoarse singing of a cricket. I put the box down on the ground, pointed at it and fired three shots. When the echo of the final shot had dissipated there was an astonishing silence. And then, suddenly, a burst of machine-gun fire, to my left, disturbed the night. For a moment I was paralyzed with dread, then I turned back toward the jeep and started to run. Behind me, above the roar of the shooting, I could distinctly hear Leopoldino's dry laughter.

My friend was already at the wheel:

"Man, get a move on! Hard luck, looks like you started a war . . ."

As we plunged speedily into the night, headlights off, he turned toward me:

"Did you kill the creature, then?"

I answered with a grunt. All I wanted was to get out of there.

"Had to be done," said my friend, and his smile shone in the darkness. "The guy knew too much . . ."

The Green Beetle

A FEW MONTHS ago, I published a piece in Brazil's *Globo* newspaper about a young Togolese man, Thomas Agbessi, who had disappeared mysteriously from inside a police van in Málaga, having been arrested for producing fake credit cards. Unable to comprehend what had happened, the Spanish police questioned the other detainees, also African, who were still inside the vehicle. These lads told a story that didn't convince the Spaniards: at a given point in the journey, Thomas had stripped naked, whereupon he'd hugged his friends, invoked his ancestors, and "disappeared mystically," like an agile and imponderable African Houdini.

Some days later, I got a Facebook message from an Angolan who claimed to have witnessed the miracle. He too, he assured me, had been in that Spanish police van. Released owing to a lack of evidence, he'd traded Málaga for Lisbon. We arranged to meet at Camões Square, by the statue of the poet. I arrived early. I sat on a bench to watch the tourists. Twenty minutes went by. Then a young man sat down beside me. He was very thin, with little spiky braids, and a fragile look about him, yet simultaneously very determined, almost fierce.

"You do seem younger like this, in flesh," he said in a soft voice, with a lovely Benguela accent.

"In *the* flesh," I corrected him.

"Right, in the flesh. In the photos you were angrier."

We sat at one of the tables of a small street kiosk, drinking mazagran and savoring their delicate dough pasties. We talked about Angola, the political changes underway, and the feeling how none of those changes were improving the lives of those who were least protected. Finally, I asked him about Agbessi:

"And what about Thomas, where did he get to?"

The young man shrugged:

"Ah, but you should be asking: Thomas, all of us, those of us who were in that police car, where had we come *from*? That's the right question to ask."

I looked at him, in stunned silence. "From suffering," the young man said, answering his own question. "Disappearing's easy. We disappear a lot, us Africans. We've always been well-trained at disappearing. Appearing inside that van, that was the hard part. Some of them crossed the desert to get here. Days in the sun. Nights in the cold. Nothing to eat, almost nothing to drink. And then the sea, on speedboats, if you fall in the water you die – can you imagine? That's how they lived, afraid, always afraid, very, very afraid, till they landed in Spain."

He fell silent. He finished his mazagran. When he got excited, the little braids jumped and stood up on his head as if they had a life of their own. And what about him, how had he gotten to Spain? The young man smiled:

"By train, from Lisbon. And Lisbon I came to by plane. My family all pitched in to pay for my flight. I wanted to study, but I couldn't get into the university. A friend told me in Málaga there'd be some great work. So I went. All I found was slave labor. Well, so be it, a slave is what I was. One evening I was in a square, chatting to my friends, and the police came and took us away."

As we were talking, five lads arrived carrying drums, guitars and other musical instruments. They set up two microphones and started to sing.

"I know this one," said the young man. "My dad used to sing it to me, when I was a boy."

I smiled. Any Angolan my age knew that song.

"And Thomas?" I insisted. "How'd he get out of the van?"

"He didn't get out. He just disappeared."

"What do you mean?"

"It's like I said. Disappearing's easy. Those Portuguese, they look and don't see us."

"So Thomas was in the van when the police opened the doors?"

"Of course. The police opened the doors, we got out, and Thomas got out with us. He walked right past the police, completely naked, and took off. He left."

"Invisible?"

"Invisible."

He looked at me, quite serious, while I digested this information. Then he took a matchbox out of his pants pocket and put it on the table:

"He left me this."

I took the box and opened it. Inside there gleamed the carcass of a green beetle.

"How beautiful! A beetle?"

"His childhood!"

I didn't answer. If you've never hidden a river in your pants pocket it's because you've never been a little boy. A river, a rare feather, a sunset, the brilliance of a firefly, a plastic cowboy with a hole in his chest, a green beetle. The band was now playing Mbirin-Mbirin. Two girls, very tall and very blonde, were holding each other and dancing, in slow abandon.

"So Thomas just went off onto the street invisible?"

"Invisible!" the young Benguelan confirmed, impassive, calming his rebellious braids with his right hand. "He'd had a lot of practice."

"And what are you going to do with his childhood?"

"I'm going to keep it. I'm the safety deposit box. Perhaps one day he'll come back."

Open to the Breeze

THE SIGN caught my eye: "The Last Supper – Restaurant – 7km." I stopped the car. The sign was pointing toward a small beaten-earth road, which disappeared between the tall coconut palms, in the direction of the dunes. I was hungry. And besides, I was curious to meet a person capable of baptizing a restaurant with that name.

I understood the reason for the name when, moments before spotting the restaurant, I came across a small cemetery: some dozen gravestones scattered about in the lacy shade of the coconut palms. The restaurant was fifty meters or so further on, up on top of the dunes. It was a wooden house, painted sky blue and supported on stilts, with a large veranda running all the way around it. Inside there were only two tables, and not a single chair. A very tall man, thin and prickly as a cactus, was sitting on the balcony reading a newspaper. He stood up unhurriedly and held out his hand:

"A very good afternoon to you!"

"Good afternoon! Are you still serving lunch?"

The man smiled sadly:

"I'm sorry to say, we no longer serve meals. The business has shut down. But we're open to the breeze."

I thanked him. On the part of the veranda that was facing the sea, there were four chairs. I sat on one of them, looking not toward the smooth waters, set aflame by a vast sun, but inward into myself. Nothing but scrub, my ex-wife used to say to me. On the inside you're nothing but wild bushland. To her, that was an insult. She would look into my eyes and see my rugged and inhospitable soul, an enormous stretch of open country, impossible to cultivate or develop. I, however, always thought that line was an overly generous compliment. I would like to be all scrubland inside.

The man sat down beside me. He introduced himself:

"Tarcísio. Tarcísio Joy." He pointed behind him, with that slow, elegant way he had of moving. "Did you see the gravestones?"

I confirmed that I had. It was impossible to get to the restaurant without passing the little cemetery. Tarcísio explained that all its dead were relatives of his. The coconut grove belonged to the family. The house had been built by his maternal grandmother.

"Did she die?" I asked.

"No," said Tarcísio, seriously. "She evaporated. She was much too

160

polite just to die all of a sudden. My grandmother didn't want us to suffer. So she disappeared very gradually."

His grandmother had fallen asleep on the hammock where they had laid her, right here, on the blue veranda. At first, she still answered the questions her children and grandchildren addressed to her. She would give these tiny little laughs whenever anyone said to her, *grandmother's on fire today*. Finally she only had the strength to summon up a gentle smile. I'm still here, that's what her smile was saying, and that small brightness lit up the afternoon.

Tarcísio told me all this in a voice that was gentle and warm, which didn't seem to be coming from his mouth but from the very heart of the house. After his grandmother evaporated, her children and grandchildren scattered. He alone remained. His grandmother had taught him to cook. She had left him a recipe book. Transforming the house into a restaurant had been his way of remaining there. He hadn't had much luck. The restaurant was far from the big cities. Only the most bewildered of outsiders, like me, showed up there.

"For you to find me, you must first be lost yourself," said Tarcísio, rigid and solemn as an ancient prophet.

"Do you not want a partner?" I asked.

Tarcísio looked at me, amazed. He gave a happy laugh:

"OK, you don't need to be quite *that* lost!"

"I'm serious! I've got money in the bank. Savings. We'll have some work done on the place, and reopen the restaurant. In exchange, all I want is for you to give me one of the bedrooms. And a plot in the cemetery for when I die."

"Do you have any plans to die?"

I shrugged: "Dying well is one of my life plans."

I was hiding the truth: I wasn't expecting to make any money from this business. What I wanted was to practice my natural talent for being scrubland. I wanted my ex-wife to look into my eyes one day and say:

"There's so much scrub in you, you can no longer even see the road."

That was how I came to be the owner of half of a blue restaurant, in a place with no name or mailing address. Tarcísio cooks every day. I get the tables ready, but nobody ever shows up. We have lunch on the veranda, sitting opposite each other. We talk little. In the evening I go down to the cemetery, stretch out on the ground, shut my eyes, and feel the scrubland flourishing within me.

The Outrageous Baobab

THE SO-CALLED Baobab Highway, which stretches right across the whole municipality of Chongoroi, in Angola's Benguela province, is much used by heavy trucks carrying goods to Lubango. That was where it all began. One afternoon, an old truck driver, Justino Paciência Mango, better known as Juju, pulled his vehicle over and got out to relieve his bladder. It was then that he saw it, the baobab tree, standing no more than thirty meters from the highway. He approached it, unable to believe his own eyes: on the side of the vast tree trunk there opened up an outrageous vulva.

Juju laughed. He took a few photos of the unusual phenomenon with his phone, and sent them to various workmates and friends. Within a month, the baobab had become a compulsory stopping-point for the drivers, who took advantage of the opportunity to stretch their legs, exchanging jokes and photographing themselves in front of that vast vegetal representation of the origin of the world.

A few weeks later, stalls selling snacks and drinks started cropping up around the tree.

Pastor Lívio Passarinho, from the Church of the Holy Sacrifice, learned of this business from one of the truck-drivers' wives, who – disgusted – held out her phone for him to see, presenting him with a frontal nude of the outrageous baobab. Passarinho immediately understood what they were dealing with: this was the mocking finger of the devil.

The Brazilian had arrived in Angola two months earlier, with three other pastors from Rio, and had managed in just a few short months to assemble a legion of devout followers. In Chongoroi he found an extraordinary "lewd circus" underway, as he explained in a message to the bishop of his congregation. In desperation, he began by carrying out an exorcism on the baobab, to which it protested most vociferously, in good Latin, Aramaic and Umbundu, while nevertheless refusing to hide the prodigious obscenity. The exorcism had the effect of attracting even more people. By now, the tree's fame had spread right across the country. A film crew came from Luanda, intending to shoot a porn movie in that location. Passarinho enlisted a group of fifty of the faithful, who surrounded the obscene trunk, and, chanting, faced up to the director's fury and the jeers of three muscular actors, two of whom were totally naked.

That night, the pastor suffered a dream. Jesus appeared to him upon a winged horse, and without saying a word, threw a blue dress into his arms, before flying off into the distance. Next morning, the Brazilian went in search of a tailor. The man he chose was Anastácio Corte Real, a calm guy, of few words, who'd had one of his legs eaten by war, and who, since that time, had set up a workshop in Cazenga.

Anastácio showed no surprise at the commission. It is true he had never dressed a tree before, let alone a baobab, but, as he explained calmly, "there's a first time for everything." He wanted to meet the customer. He went with a stepladder and two assistants. He took the measurements. He returned a fortnight later with a beautiful dress, in bright colors, a strapless number that was a perfect fit for the baobab's body, hanging without a single crease almost all the way down to the ground.

The garment was not popular with the truck drivers, nor with the sellers of food and drink. The latter, however, quickly reconciled themselves to it, since the tree continued to attract curious visitors, some naked, some clothed.

It was then that one of the faithful found a second proudly sexed baobab, and out came Anastácio from Luanda once again, under contract to produce another oversized dress. Next, another lady reported the existence, in a nearby wood, of a mulemba tree, or rather, of a mulembo in the masculine form of the noun, priapic and exhibitionist, a true affront to traditional values and Christian morality, for which the tailor designed a magnificent pair of pants, in the classic style, transforming the tree into a respectable old-fashioned gentleman.

Before long, Chongoroi boasted more dressed trees than undressed ones. Pastor Lívio Passarinho began to have lewd dreams about mango and avocado trees. Any naked tree would arouse wicked thoughts in him. If it hadn't been for the intervention of the civil authorities, who arrested and deported him, disbanding the church, Passarinho would have dressed every forest in the country, including the Mayombe.

Anastácio learned of Passarinho's deportation with a certain relief. He was tired of dressing trees. Today, in his workshop, over in Cazenga, he dresses exclusively people. Only very large people, but still people.

The President's Madness

T HE NEWS caught the whole world off guard – the president of the United States of America had had a fall, after choking on a cookie, and was in a coma. For two weeks, the powerful U.S.A. came to a halt, gripped, hanging on each new medical report. And then the president opened his eyes and started to speak. To speak? Well, the report was cautious:

"The president opened his eyes and attempted to communicate."

That afternoon, in a brief press conference, the journalists launched themselves like rabid dogs onto the spokesman for the medical team:

"What does 'attempted to communicate' mean?"

The man, a peaceable sort of fellow, with a white beard, balding, sought to calm people's spirits:

"The president is conscious, he seems to recognize people and is capable of articulating some sounds. However, it is too early to offer any prognoses. We can't yet know whether he suffered any irreversible damage in some part of the brain that is responsible for speech."

That night, a major TV network broadcast a bit of amateur footage, with no sound and only a shaky picture, in which the president could be seen sitting up in bed, speaking – or rather, we ought to correct ourselves, *attempting to communicate*. What was remarkable was that he was attempting to communicate with all the self-confidence of a healthy man, gesturing with his hands, troubled, possibly even angry, and all the while, standing opposite him, his wife, the secretary of defense and an unidentified advisor looked on with a mixture of terror and astonishment. What could he have been saying? In the studio, an expert lip-reader was unable to explain the mystery:

"That's not English," he stated categorically. "Not even *his* English."

He said this and became anxious. The news anchor couldn't suppress a laugh. Everyone in America knew that their president regularly disrespected his mother tongue. The more critical voices suggested that this twisted syntax corresponded to some equally twisted thought processes, or even an absence of thought altogether – but that had never been scientifically proven. Stranger still: the president spoke no other language other than English. (His English being to the real thing as fast food is to fine cuisine.) So the footage of the president energetically babbling away gave birth to all kinds of speculations.

"He's gone nuts," the most reasonable ones were saying.

"He's been kidnapped by extraterrestrials," others swore, "and brainwashed and sent back to earth. The aliens are now trying to communicate with us through him."

This latter theory might have prevailed were it not for Dona Florinda Silva, one of the cleaning staff, on coming into the presidential room one afternoon to carry out the task that had been allocated to her, having surprised the most powerful man in the world in a desperate monologue with his psychiatrist.

"The *cabrão's* speaking Portuguese! *Carago!* And it's from up in Miragaia."

The president of the United States of America had indeed spent days trying to make himself understood by his family, his doctors, secretaries of state, advisers, in competent Portuguese – and with a lavish Porto accent! He did not know himself, however, which language it was. He needed to be shown where Portugal was on a map. The president became angry:

"*Mas vossemecês acham que eu sou algum morcão?!*"

It wasn't easy for him to accept that he could only express himself in a distant little dialect, part-Latin and part-Arab, spoken by a handful of Spaniards in a tiny little rectangle on the fringes of Europe. They explained to him that, no, Mr. President, Portuguese is the sixth most widely spoken language in the world. Brazilians speak Portuguese, too, and so do some African peoples. The news consoled him a little, even if it still wasn't as good as speaking like a person:

"*E quando recomeço a falar como uma pessoa?!*"

Nobody could give him that reassurance – maybe he'd stay that way for good? The neurosurgeons didn't even know how come he was able to communicate in a language he had never studied. The knock on his head, some believe, had activated his pre-birth memory (the president's mother had spent four months in the Unvanquished City while pregnant). In any case, the fact raised a number of extremely delicate questions. For example: could a guy who didn't speak a word of English be considered a U.S. citizen and occupy the White House? And what was the president now, in ethnic terms – Hispanic? North-West Portuguese?

The Portuguese-speaking world was split. While the Angolan government was pleased at the news – "A Lusophone president in the White House will undoubtedly help to tighten the bonds between our two great nations" – Portugal sought to dodge the controversial subject:

"To prevent anybody from thinking that we might be responding to the American president's tragedy with any kind of nationalistic jingoism, the Portuguese president is going to start to speak only English from now on. Utah English."

The Brazilians, meanwhile, were not impressed:

"The guy's speaking Portuguese?" said one employee at their ministry of foreign affairs, amazed. "With that accent, I thought it was Russian."

This lasted two and a half months. Then, one fine morning, the American president woke up speaking Efik, an Afro-Cuban Creole from an all-male secret religious society, Abakuá. In Havana, the Cuban leader remarked:

"You know, I always suspected he wasn't as stupid as he seemed."

The Unbelievable yet True Story of D. Nicolau Água-Rosada

"Truth in History is not what happened, but what having been able to be, seems to have been."

—SEVERINO DE SOUZA, *A Brief History of the Angolan Peoples*

"News has reached us from Ambriz that the young prince of Kongo, D. Nicolau Água-Rosada, has been barbarically murdered by a raging mob. We have learned that the heathens of the region attacked an English trading post in Quissembo, a place where D. Nicolau was taking refuge, kidnapping the unfortunate young man, whom they later killed with blows from their machetes (jungle knives), chopping off his limbs and carrying away his head in triumph on a spike. We await confirmation of this news." —OFFICIAL BULLETIN, 25 MARCH 1857

THE LEAFLET was garnet-red and it announced in stirring and artful rhetoric an extraordinary spectacle of recreational physics, to be presented this Sunday at the Providence Theater. In smaller type, the ladies and gentlemen of Luanda were notified that the same spectacle would be repeated a week later, this time in the spacious and welcoming home of the firm *Carnegie & Co.*

D. Nicolau Água-Rosada e Sardónia read the leaflet without feeling any particular enthusiasm, so far was he from knowing that this advertisement would change his destiny. That Sunday he decked himself out to perfection and in the evening he headed to the theater, where he enjoyed himself much more than he had expected, marveling at the strange wonders of Professor Jácome Ulysses Jr. The professor was a small man, yellow and withered, but his exuberance of gesture, enormous twisted mustache, and Brazilian accent lent him an uncommon vivacity. He introduced his act as being totally original, never before seen anywhere in the world, with the exception of Paris, naturally, and having its basis in the physical-chemical experiments of Webber.

"The phenomenon you are about to witness, my most worthy guests, is not the work of demiurges nor of magicians; it is the product of many years of scientific study, of endless toil and labor on the chemistry of chloroform." The chemist's voice went up a notch:

"Illustrious ladies, illustrious gentlemen, what I am about to show you now, you will never forget."

And he set about explaining how, through his researches into chloroform, he had reached an understanding of the state of drowsiness, and developed a process capable of inducing this state in people or animals, lightening their bodies to such an extent that it was possible thereby to attain their suspension in the ether, vertically or horizontally.

When he reached this point, the physicist had his daughter, a slender, delicate girl, come up onto the stage, and she sniffed the liquid in a little blue bottle he had in his pocket. The girl fell instantly asleep, but rather than collapsing to the floor in a rustle of silks, she remained on her feet, motionless, while her father continued to shake the blue vial.

In expansive but slow movements he did this until all the liquid had evaporated. Then, he took hold of the girl by the waist and raised her into the air. Against all logic, when he let go of her, the delicate little figure remained where she was, floating twenty centimeters off the ground. There was the sound of some nervous laughter, applause, and various expressions of approval. Smiling, the physicist asked for silence, and took hold of the girl, spinning her in the air. Finally he left her lying there, floating almost a meter over the floor.

"Now," he said, furnishing himself with an iron hoop, "it is essential that I make it absolutely clear that there is no kind of trickery in this experiment. There are no transparent wires, strings, or threads. Merely chloroform, ladies and gentlemen, only things that can be explained by science."

And then, slowly, he passed the young woman's body through the iron hoop. The whole hall rose in a thundering ovation. D. Nicolau, stiff in his new morning suit, stood too. The truth was, he'd never seen anything like it. When the show was over, he went over to Ezequiel de Souza to be introduced to the distinguished scientist. De Souza at that time was one of the richest traders in the city. He had been responsible for the Brazilian's journey to Luanda, paying for his crossing and putting him up in his house. At that moment he was swelling up conceitedly, surrounded by the excited buzz of a group of gentlemen and young ladies, all of them wanting to get to know Jácome Jr. better. When Nicolau's turn came, the trader introduced him as the prince of Kongo, the son of King Henrique II, and it seemed to the young man as though a gleam of uncommon interest appeared in the Brazilian's eyes. It wasn't long before they found themselves in pleasant conversation, with the scientist wanting to know everything about Angola, asking questions Nicolau was at times unable to answer.

As it was a splendid night, they went to the esplanade of the Café Bijou where, amid beers and amusing anecdotes, the young prince ended up leading the foreigner down the bumpy paths of Kongo's royal genealogy. D. Nicolau Água-Rosada e Sardónia was in fact the son of Henrique II, crowned king of Kongo on the thirteenth of January, 1844, as stated in the relevant act of acclamation, and according to the royal charter of recognition, signed by her majesty Dona Maria. With the death of the monarch, and in conformity with local laws, his nephew, D. Pedro VI, with the approval of his majesty the king of Portugal, D. Luís I, succeeded him to the throne.

Dona Maria was still alive when Nicolau was handed over by his parents into the care of a Portuguese captain, António Joaquim de Castro, who brought him to Lisbon. In that city, the young boy learned the first letters of his alphabet, some basics of French, and all the arts befitting a gentleman, from horse-riding to fencing. When, eight years later, he returned to Angola, he was an altogether different person from the one who had left and couldn't imagine ever coming to appreciate the habits and customs of his people, hence his decision to remain in Luanda, where he didn't find it hard to secure himself a position at the Council of the Exchequer. His good work and his abilities meant that he was promoted to a clerical position, and, in 1857, he was dispatched to fill the post of clerk to the Council of the Exchequer in the Ambriz region.

At the point at which his destiny crossed paths (irremediably) with that of Professor Jácome Jr., Nicolau was passing through

Luanda, where he had stopped off with the intention of visiting some friends. He was a tall, very dark-skinned young Black man, pleasant of face and agreeable of manner, little given to the carousing that suited his age, and whom nobody had ever known to allow himself to get involved in trouble, political or otherwise. His refusal to return to São Salvador de Kongo, to occupy the place that fell to him in the governance of the kingdom, had aroused his own people's hatred against him. But otherwise he had no known enemies.

Professor Jácome Jr. listened to Nicolau's tale with focused attention. He asked about specific details, his questions multiplying. He seemed particularly interested in learning what Nicolau thought about the autonomist ideas that, at that time, were starting to liven up Luandan conversations. The young man had never been especially excited by the subject but he knew that many of the city's distinguished gentlemen were involved in it, most of all the rich traders unhappy at the way the metropolis was governing the colony.

They said their goodbyes at daybreak. Jácome Jr. reminded D. Nicolau that he would be repeating his act in a week and insisted that he come. This time the performance would be taking place for a select audience at the residence known as *Bungo House*, belonging to the English firm *Carnegie & Co*, where it was traditional for the English community and the best Luanda families to fraternize in lively evenings filled with music and plays. Some of those who frequented the house had even set up a theater group, the Shakespeare Dramatic Society, that would stage his plays in both English and Portuguese.

On the Sunday, Bungo House was heaving with people. Playing hostess was the wife of the British vice-consul, an extremely beautiful woman whose face was lit by a permanent smile. D. Nicolau, who had never before had the privilege of visiting this residence, was shy and fearful, astonished by the glare of the chandeliers and the elegance of the couples, afraid that not having received any kind of formal invitation, his presence there might be considered inappropriate. He was already regretting having listened to the Brazilian physicist, a man he barely knew and who had only invited him to visit Bungo House after having had a lot to drink. He calmed down when Jácome Jr. arrived with the house's owner, William Newton, and the two men came over to him with no apparent awkwardness, seemingly delighted to have him there.

The evening couldn't have gone better: William Newton played some popular Irish songs on his flute; the graduate Alfredo Trony showed off his conjuring skills, and the beautiful Maria José Falcão sang, very well, some pieces of opera. To conclude, Professor Jácome Jr. repeated his wondrous act, but this time, and because the audience was urging him on so enthusiastically, another three girls fell asleep. One of them must have been particularly light, however, either that or the physicist overdid the application of his concoction: having fallen into a deep sleep, the girl did not merely hover, like the others, but began steadily to rise in the air, slowly and dangerously she climbed, grazing the sharp flames of the living room's heavy chandeliers until she was finally stopped by the high carved mahogany ceiling, from where she could only be rescued with the help of a stepladder. If the curious experiment had been carried out in the open air, the young woman would now be sailing in a puffed-out colorful dress among the stars.

Colonel Arcénio de Carpo, who allowed himself to be easily enchanted by all kinds of novelty, was determined to unearth the secret of the Brazilian scientist's concoction, no matter what it took:

"A discovery of this nature should not be limited to entertaining audiences," he explained excitedly, "it could have incalculable practical applications."

And he was already picturing a population of nefelibatas, building, amid the clouds, arched rainbows of light and water; fantastical transparent castles; immense staircases, capable of connecting the Earth to the lunar star.

Once the show was over, D. Nicolau got ready to leave, dazed by all the wonders of that long and memorable night. Yet before he was able to say goodbye to anybody at all, William Newton took him by the arm and led him to a parlor on the second floor, where the young man was surprised to find the vice-consul of the United Kingdom, in the company of Ezequiel de Souza and another African gentleman. The three of them were calmly smoking, cross-legged, but no sooner had they seen him than they were up, holding their hands out to him. William Newton was still doing the introductions when the Brazilian professor came in, red-faced. He was the one who, with much coughing, explained to the Kongolese man why they had brought him there.

"We know you have never been drawn to politics," Jácome Jr. began. "Yet a gentleman like you, senhor, in whose veins the noblest blood of Africa is flowing, cannot remain removed from the great stage of History. A gentleman like you, senhor, whose generosity is well known to all, cannot remain deaf to the cries of his own people! A gentleman like you has an obligation, nay, a moral duty, to declare himself publicly and categorically against all the humiliations, the extortions and the violences that the Portuguese have been perpetrating in the Kongo region."

And the Brazilian got more and more exited, his face flushing redder and redder, in a crescendo of rage that seemed to entertain the vice-consul, and at which the two Angolans smilingly approved. D. Nicolau, meanwhile, had shrunk back in his chair, frightened by the little physicist's stentorian verbosity and the delicacy of the situation. When he finally spoke, it was only to remind the distinguished gentlemen, shyly, that he had moved away, of his own free will, from the political struggle, not thinking it right therefore that he should now involve himself in matters about which he had no detailed knowledge.

Jácome Jr. struck him down with a look:

"Detailed knowledge? We're not talking to you about details, senhor! What we want is for you to join us in the fight against the spurious claims of the Portuguese, that miserable sub-race of slavers, of slave traders, of slavagists . . ."

And then, making a great effort to control himself, he asked one of the Africans present, Lima da Alfândega, to explain to Nicolau what was expected of him.

"It's simple," said the Angolan, a mulatto man who was still young, with small round glasses and a wide chickpea head, "you could go to London to make a claim before the British courts of the rights that are due to you over the Kingdom of Kongo and its dependencies. It is well known that Portugal illegally occupied the whole region from Ambriz to Molembo. Now, England is inclined to support a formal claim against this state of things, with the certainty that many other nations would share identical feelings of justice. With strong international support, Senhor Nicolau, you might even be able to demand the independence of the entire Kingdom of Kongo, begetting . . . so we believe . . . a broader movement of revolt against Portugal's intolerable control."

And the mulatto went on with his speech, assuring the astonished clerk that a lot of Luanda traders had already confirmed their backing for such a scheme, and there was now nothing preventing it from being put into practice but the absence of one single person: him, D. Nicolau Água-Rosada.

The prince pulled out a handkerchief and nervously wiped his sweat-beaded face.

"This all seems crazy to me," he managed to say in a mere wisp of a voice. "And how am I supposed to get to Great Britain?"

It was the vice-consul's turn to give a magnificent smile. If his excellency were to accept the idea, the British crown would be most proud to put a warship at his disposal. Of course, it would be best to maintain the greatest secrecy around the whole matter until the Prince of Kongo's arrival in London had been accomplished. Fortunately the Angolan coast was vast and barely watched; it would be easy to arrange D. Nicolau's boarding of the ship, even around Ambriz. The unfortunate clerk didn't have time to add another word. Jácome Jr. had already opened a bottle of fizz and was filling their glasses.

"My dear senhores," he was shouting enthusiastically, "let us drink to the health of his excellency, the future King of a free Kongo!"

He raised his glass and the other men copied his movement. Twenty-eight days later, on a hot, clear Sunday in March, D. Nicolau found himself en route to Quissembo, a place he hadn't visited since his boyhood and where *Carnegie & Co.* held an important trading outpost. He was, per their agreement, to wait there for the arrival of a warship under the British flag. He was filled with fear, and his reasons for this fear were not unfounded. The previous day, when he had revealed to a colleague, an Exchequer treasurer, that he planned to take a trip to Quissembo, the other man had been greatly alarmed, making him see just how problematic such a journey would be, given that the people from the north of Ambriz had not looked kindly on him since he had quit Kongo to go live in close collusion with the whites. Now, stretched out in his palanquin, which was being carried jerkily down the paths that wound through the bush-land, D. Nicolau regretted not having followed his colleague's advice. The whole thing was a huge mistake. He never should have allowed himself to become entangled in such an adventure, or, at the very least, have agreed to board ship in Quissembo.

From time to time he shot an anxious glance into the dark, dense forest, afraid that he would see his father's warriors leaping out, yelling ferociously. On several occasions he ordered the palanquin to stop so that one of the bearers might check the conditions of the road up ahead. They could already make out the roof of the English trading post, and the young man's heart was just starting to calm down when they heard, distant but piercing, the grim laughter of a band of Humbi. As he entered the trading post, where a smiling William Newton awaited him, D. Nicolau was a man without hope.

Nobody ever found out who it was that had informed the people of Kongo of the presence, in Quissembo, of the traitor prince. What is known is that on that same night, a large troop of men surrounded the trading post, heatedly demanding D. Nicolau's head. William Newton came to the door in conciliatory mood but was met with insults and threats. The prince, shouted the Kongolese, had fallen into a big conspiracy and now needed to be judged by the laws of his people. The Englishman refused to satisfy their request.

"D. Nicolau," said Newton, trying to fool the mob, "left on a warship this morning."

These words only served to enrage the already over-excited spirits. Some of the men had lit torches and approached with them, saying they were going to set fire to the trading post if D. Nicolau was not handed over. Immense in his British dignity, William Newton withdrew inside and ordered that the flag be raised. Then, in a single movement of fury, as sudden and irrepressible as a gust of wind, the crowd surged forward, breaking everything, knocking down doors and crashing through walls.

D. Nicolau Água-Rosada, who had taken refuge at the rear of the building, heard the din and, seized by panic, jumped out a window into the yard. Feeling as though his body was already being dismembered with machete blows, he launched off on a run through the orange, papaya, and guava trees, until he crashed hard into the high wall that surrounded the property. Desperate, hearing the uproar approaching, he remembered the gift that, on their parting, Jácome Jr. had bestowed upon him. Trembling violently, he reached into the right-hand pocket of his jacket and pulled out a small blue glass bottle.

The first rebels who reached the wall found nothing there, except a little glass vial on the ground. Then one of them raised his eyes to the sky and gave a cry of amazement. Against the vast light, round and white like a silver coin, was the fragile silhouette of a man. Serenely, like a wrecked ship amid algae and corals, D. Nicolau was sleeping. And rising, ever upward.

The Good Despot

VERY OFTEN, invariably after one of those abundant Saturday lunches that stretch out almost to dusk, I hear businessmen, generals and some of my ministers recalling the hardships of the past: "When I was a kid, I was always eating quicuerra." Anybody hearing them, their eyes shining with emotion, lost in their distant childhoods, would think they actually missed the quicuerra they ate for breakfast, lunch and dinner. Many of them say being at the table of an expensive restaurant doesn't sit well with them – or they don't sit well in those restaurants, as one of them puts it. They prefer to eat barbecue with their hands in the poorest of slum yards.

They probably still eat quicuerra in secret remembering the wretchedness they suffered in the days of the colony. As for me, I never went hungry. I never ate quicuerra just to fool my stomach. I ate quicuerra because I liked the mixture of peanut with the manioc flour and the sugar. I don't feel nostalgic about anything.

I'm lying. I do sometimes feel some nostalgia for playing the guitar. I used to play guitar with some conviction. So much so that I earned the nickname Franco, in tribute to François Luambo Makiadi, known as Franco, who in those days, in the late fifties, was already a great success in Léopoldville heading up the legendary OK Jazz. Groups in Luanda had names that were round and rhythmic: Quimbandas of Rhythm, Negoleiros of Rhythm, Africa Rhythms, Snipe Hunting, N'Goma Jazz, Merengues, Ases do Prenda, or Tropical Semba.

When I say I feel some nostalgia for playing the guitar, I don't mean that I miss playing it per se, if I wanted to pick it up I'd just have somebody buy one, one that belonged to Franco, for example, or John Lennon, and I'd hire Paulinho da Viola as a teacher, until my fingers began to dance again. What I miss is playing the guitar with no past and no future. I used to play like somebody flying, and it was the pure joy of the music, the girls spinning, spinning, with their high-heeled shoes, their colored dresses, their straightened hair, and their eyes locked on mine, the strong smell of pomade and cheap perfume.

When we're on a stage, people notice us. That, after all, is what stages are for. Women noticed me. Men noticed that women were noticing me, and that was how I got into politics. I got into politics because I was on a stage playing guitar and women noticed me.

When we talked about the Congo, we didn't just talk about

Franco. We talked about Franco loudly, and about Lumumba in hushed voices. One day, after whispering about Lumumba, and about how afraid the Belgians were of him, another guitarist, with whom I used to play, wanted to know my opinion on Angola's independence. Up till the moment he asked me that question, I'd never given it any thought. My friend smiled (he smiled better than he played) and told me that one day Angola would have a black president. Maybe it was because of my friend's smile, maybe because the night was warm and gentle and filled with stars, and the beer was cold and good, whatever it was, the idea entranced me. That night, I couldn't sleep.

Every day I felt, in my skin, the humiliation of the colonial system. I only needed to take a cab. Hard to believe today, but back then, in Luanda, taxi drivers were all white. Most of them very racist. I'm remembering a Luís Visconde song that recounts the argument between a passenger and a taxi driver: "The scowling driver soon replied, / You'll have to walk to see your chicks. / Don't think that I'll share my ride, / Just so you can get your kicks."

We left the house and we were in a foreign country. Any child could see the injustice we lived in. And yet, it never occurred to me, as it did not to so many others, that it could ever be different. From that night, I started to imagine what Angola would be like without the Portuguese. Any change has its beginning with somebody, probably someone who hasn't got a job, imagining a change. One should not give the masses the means, that is, the education, nor the time, to hone and release their fantasies. The ideal is for the masses to be entirely occupied with survival. Young students, who are precisely people trained to think and imagine, and who have time available for such things, constitute a terrible threat to strong governments. I dream of a country with no students.

On February 4th 1961, around two hundred nationalists, armed with katanas, attacked the Military Penitentiary with the aim of liberating a group of political prisoners. Forty were killed then and there. In the days that followed, many more people died. The colonizers went into the poor neighborhoods guns blazing. A black man who was protesting in public for some reason or other – for example, because he'd seen a white man cutting in line – was immediately labeled a terrorist and beaten up. Beating up black people became a kind of sport for the colonial bourgeoisie. I was troubled by it all. I started thinking about leaving Angola to join one of the nationalist movements.

I went to talk to my friend – the one who knew how to smile. He listened to me politely, and smiled, and then asked me two or three questions, trying to assess the firmness of my convictions. Finally he showed me a pamphlet for the MPLA. I didn't know who the MPLA were. I'd heard of the UPA, of Holden Roberto. I'd heard about a white priest, whom they'd accused of leading the attack on the Military Penitentiary. This priest (so it was murmured) was linked to the UPA. I'd heard of various other movements. But nothing about the MPLA.

"The MPLA is the people's vanguard," said my friend. "The UPA is a tribalist movement, made up of backward people. The MPLA represents all progressive Angolans, regardless of tribe."

Two months later, if that, I was already in Matadi, in the Congo. I found the movement divided into several factions. I understood what a risk it would be to associate myself with any one of them. Those different factions would devour one another, to the delight of the UPA and the Portuguese colonials and, later, of all our countless internal and external enemies.

Some time later, an opportunity arose for me to study in Moscow, at the Patrice Lumumba People's Friendship University, established in 1960 to provide high-quality education to the future leaders of the so-called Third World. I accepted right away. I wanted to fight for independence, but not through the barrel of a gun. The first time I was given a weapon, in Matadi, I understood that I would never be a guerrilla. That furious iron (the legendary AK-47), weighing heavy in my hands, filled me with sheer horror.

Moscow proved a good choice. I met many interesting people. I remember one Venezuelan man, a bit of a rebel, by the name of

Ilich. He had two brothers: one was called Vladimir, and the other, Lenin. Their father, of course, was a fully committed Marxist. Ilich liked parties. He knew how to get hold of the best vodka and he was always in the company of beautiful women, blonde and dark, with long legs and angel faces (bad teeth, though). I never really liked vodka. Vodka to me was just a way of getting close to women.

Ilich asked me a lot of questions about the armed struggle in Angola. He wanted to fight. He longed to get involved in the revolution – any revolution – so long as he could machine-gun counter-revolutionaries and blow up bombs. As for me, violence appalled me more and more. I kept extending my studies, delaying the call to the forests. Looking back, I'm sure I did the right thing. I brought some happiness into the lives of countless Soviet women, in an internationalist ardor of which I can be proud, while at the same time learning to hide my thoughts. I became skilled in this intimate exercise. So skilled that often even I myself don't know what I think about a particular subject.

Today, my friend Ilich, who has become known across the world by the name Carlos the Jackal, is getting old with no honor and no glory, in a high-security prison, in the outskirts of Paris. I, meanwhile, am getting rich. In a way, one might see this as a triumph of non-violence.

My grandmother used to say these words that should be a point of compulsory reflection in every school of diplomacy: "Never speak so well of anybody that you can't then speak ill of them later. Never speak so ill of anybody that you can't then speak well of them later."

I dedicated myself to honing this life principle, until it had been summarized into two words: "Never speak!"

Silence disorients your opponents, since in the inconstant world of politics there are only ever opponents. Those people we affectionately call "comrades," or "supporters," are merely opponents who, at any given moment, happen to be on our side. They are almost always much more dangerous when they're on our side.

On May 27th 1977, there was an uprising against the president's leadership. The coup, which enjoyed the support of the Soviet Union, was quelled in just a few hours, thanks to the intervention of Cuban troops. The president took advantage of this pretext to arrest anyone who challenged him, right and left, inside and outside of the party. Many hundreds of unfortunate individuals, thousands perhaps, were shot. Weeks earlier they had given me the task of carrying out an investigation into the possible existence of a fractionist wing in the party. I wrote a long and detailed report that has been read and reread, studied, discussed, over the decades, by political scientists, historians, linguists, experts in semiotics, philosophers, psychologists, graphologists and psychoanalysts. To this day, nobody has been able to ascertain whether I was on the fractionists' side or the president's. It is possible to maintain one's silence – a convulsive kind of silence – while still seeming verbose.

The president passed away, in Moscow, just two years later. The party gathered, amid the general dismay, to find a successor. A number of historical leaders seemed to be well placed. Yet any one of these names would represent a particular tendency. Choosing one would leave the others on the verge of a nervous breakdown. The blood of the victims of May 27th had barely dried. Comrades were looking at one another and comparing the size and hardness of their nails. They pulled their necks in. My name began to circulate. "Which side's he on?" they asked. I was very young, very silent, very alone. I was the only person nobody was afraid of. So I was the one chosen.

For the first years, I played dead. I allowed myself to be seen as a faithful heir to the deceased president and, at the same time, I was quietly freeing the fractionists who had survived the firing squads and the concentration camps. I named some of them to important roles in the government. They never caused trouble again.

The fall of the Berlin Wall happened at just the right moment. On the one hand, it allowed me to distance the occasional fanatical Marxist, those ideologically mummified troops, lost in time, who would not allow themselves to be bought, not with positions nor consumer products. On the other, it allowed me to open the country up to the joys of capitalism, to the benefit of our whole big family and of the country as a whole. The opening up to capitalism was also the first great ax-blow to the guerrilla struggle that up till that point had been supported by the United States and the international right-wing. If we unite with capitalism, why would capitalism need to fight us?

Finally, we were able, all of us, who had suffered so much for our beloved country, to begin to reap the tasty fruits of independence. I cannot understand those people who criticize us for getting rich. According to capitalist logic, to which we adhere with the purest zeal, what is to be expected of a good citizen if not that he become rich?

"Corruption!" shout the usual reactionaries. I remind these envious types that no powerful indigenous bourgeoisie has ever existed in Angola. It's true that in the first half of the nineteenth century, some urban families did get rich from the slave trade. Most, however, ended up getting poor again, following the effective abolition of slavery, at the very end of the nineteenth century, leading to what Mário Pinto de Andrade would call, with biting irony, "the Luandan lumpenaristocracy."

Our whole great effort, after the opening up to the market economy, was aimed at regenerating that same lumpenaristocracy, compensating them for what the colonial system had usurped from them – the slaves! – as well as for the foolish years of the post-independence Marxist regime. Transforming coarse workers and countryfolk into a prosperous, sophisticated bourgeoisie is a much harder operation. Yet we will get there.

I myself am connected, via some vague ancestor, to one of the oldest Luandan families. So I, too, was historically usurped, dispossessed of my slaves and of my slave-ships. How much would such an inheritance come to today?

I am similarly accused of nepotism. Or rather, I am accused of protecting my family. As I said a moment ago, in the world of politics there's no such thing as supporters, only adversaries. We cannot trust anybody, except our own children.

I only know two types of loyalty: the kind we buy, and the kind that comes from bonds of blood. The former is always volatile. You cannot trust somebody who is for sale. That is the sad paradox with which I am confronted on a daily basis – the only people I can rely on are my enemies. The concept of an enemy, I had better clarify this, is different from an adversary. An enemy is whoever cannot be bought.

The second type of loyalty, while it is very robust, can also bring unpleasant surprises. A son turning against his father seems to me the very worst of perversions, but it does happen. The safest thing, therefore, is combining the two types of loyalty, buying those who also are of our blood and sharing out the bases of political and economic power between them.

God has blessed me with many children. The hardest thing, these past years, has been managing all the egos and the jealousies. It's a delicate game. If I give one of them a private bank, I then must quickly give another a TV station. Bit by bit, I share the country out between us. Fortunately I have a country that is vast and wealthy. There is plenty to give to all my children.

The international community, and Portugal in particular, have supported, unreservedly, our model of democracy. I am equally generous toward foreigners. Many of those who only yesterday were railing against me, and against corruption, are now on my side. They've proved even cheaper to me than my adversaries. In truth, the gain is always mine.

Not that everything is perfect. Sometimes, I dream about a village I visited in the Congo, in the time of the guerrilla struggle against Portuguese colonialism. There was a lot of hunger in that region. We were received by dozens of children with swollen bellies and blue eyes. Their eyes, owing to their severe malnutrition, had lost their pigmentation. In my dream I am being pursued by thousands of blue-eyed boys. Blue light gushes from their eyes, like wild rivers, and drags everything away.

When I saw the first demonstrations of frustrated young people, never more than three hundred of them, protesting in Luanda's squares against our triumphant and original model of democracy, I remembered that dream. I studied the footage filmed by our security agents. There they were, all those irresponsible youths shouting insults, fists raised, crude placards in their hands. The angriest of them all was a singer whose father, since deceased, had worked for me. Months earlier he had dared to stop a concert, in an enclosure filled with young people, to call for the overthrow of the regime. One of my children was there. He addressed him – yes, he addressed my son! – urging him to persuade me to step down. The lad's brazenness frightened me. It frightened all my comrades. Strong regimes start to crumble when fear swaps places. I'm appalled by violence – I've said this already, and I'm quite sincere – but sometimes it's necessary to have recourse to extreme measures to prevent the onset of chaos.

I watched the footage of the protests again. I thought I recognized one of the young people taking part. He was in the squares, here and there, with a guitar on his back. He wasn't shouting. He was watching. It was his obstinate silence that bothered me the most. I gave an order for him to be followed. My head of security brought me more pieces of footage. We watched them together. I noticed his discomfort.

"Is that your son?" he asked.

I kept silent. It wasn't my son – as to that, I was certain. The following day I had the head of security dismissed and sent him, as first secretary, to an embassy in a country far away.

Since then, I've been sleeping very badly.

The Tamer of Butterflies

ANTÓNIO DE OLIVEIRA CADORNEGA was born in Vila Viçosa
in 1623, to a family of New Christians, and moved to Luanda
at the age of sixteen as a soldier. But over the course of the five
following decades he transformed, gradually, from colonizer to col-
onized: when he died at sixty-seven, he was speaking and writing
beautiful African Portuguese, enriched by countless Quimbundo
words and expressions. And he had begun to think in a way that was
magical and animist, seeing the redemptive breath of the ancestors
in all things.

"This heathen is of the belief that, with the unctures they derive
from herbs and woods, people can be transformed into lions and
into jaguars, which they call *quifumbulas*," wrote Cadornega in his
most famous work, *General History of the Angolan Wars*. In that
same book, some pages on, he recounts an episode involving a qui-
fumbula he had witnessed.

I happened upon his unpublished manuscript, *Account of the*

Wonders I Saw in Angola (1687), by sheer chance, forgotten in a pile of nineteenth-century Angolan newspapers. I'd purchased the papers for a reasonable price from an old book dealer in Recife. I had brought them home and forgotten about them. Years later, when I studied them, I found the manuscript signed by António de Oliveira Cadornega, a member of the Council of Loanda. I never had any doubts as to the document's authenticity, as the style is the same. A writer's true signature is his style.

António de Oliveira Cadornega met Queen Nzinga Mbandi, known to us as Queen Ginga; he corresponded with her, and devoted the most interesting pages of his *General History of the Angolan Wars* to her. In this manuscript, he talked about Ginga again, and about quifumbulas. According to him, one of Ginga's husbands, the chief of the Jagas – nomadic warriors who hired out their weapons to the highest bidder – had among his forces a secret unit, made up of twelve quifumbulas. These quifumbulas would attack at night, not in the commonplace reality we all share, but infiltrating the dreams of the enemy troops. The opposing soldiers would dream they were being chased by a lion, and they would awake screaming, tearing at their chests with their own nails. Not many recovered.

António de Oliveira Cadornega also describes how in the queen's court there was a senior dignitary, Nganga diá Kimbiambia, whose only role was to breed and train enormous butterflies (entomologists believe they were of the *Papilio antimachus* species), which fluttered nobly around the sovereign while she conferred with her macotas (counselors) or received emissaries from the most remote rural villages of the kingdom. When she grew weary, the queen would click her fingers, and the butterflies would cover her completely, a living curtain of the purest silk, and she, disappearing from the view of those present, would reappear wherever she chose, some miles away, or alternatively in the same place but some days earlier, or some days later.

Cadornega, who spoke Quimbundo with all the elegance of a true son of the land, had become friends with one of these butterfly tamers, a very old man by the name of Mbaxi. It is most likely that old Mbaxi initiated the ex-Portuguese man in the mysteries of breeding and training of butterflies. Cadornega suggests just this when, in his *Account of the Wonders I Saw in Angola*, he describes the journeys he took into the Angolan interior, being one morning in Luanda and the next in Muxima, a settlement several days' travel away on the back of a gnu. More significant is what he tells us in the final lines of his manuscript, preempting Albert Einstein by 268 years: "Time is no more than an ingenious trick that the Lord God has created to deceive us, since the human mind cannot conceive the appalling truth that there is no past that passes nor future that does not exist in this precise moment."

António de Oliveira Cadornega died in 1690. Or rather, he stopped being seen. One day his wife woke up and didn't find him at home. Across the city, which was very small, nobody had any word of him.

A few months ago, on the Bailundo-Bié highway, I witnessed a whirlwind of butterflies. They were yellow butterflies, at least twenty-five centimeters in wingspan, and they swirled about in the middle of the road, shining in the low, late-afternoon sunlight. I stopped the car. I saw (or thought I saw) an elusive figure dancing, half-hidden amid the boiling yellow glare. I was quite sure, at that moment, that it was my favorite seventeenth-century writer. I still am.

The Sentimental Education of the Birds

(*Jonas Savimbi speaks*)

THEY HIT ME in the back. The impact of the bullet pushed me and I fell. It feels like I'm falling still, stretched out face-down in the mud, as the morning cracks and grows around me. Moments before the attack there were birds singing in the foliage. If you opened your eyes you would see the red earth and the bright green of the grass. And thus, with my eyes closed, an almost identical landscape opens up in my memory. I listen, not to the gunshots, and there are gunshots everywhere, but to the galloping of the train. I hear it panting with its metallic effort. My heart beats in time with the machine, tam-tam, tam-tam, tam-tam, its pace increasing. A blond girl leans out of one of the windows. Her smile gives me back my breath. I keep running. The locomotive reaches the first curve. I am enveloped in a cloud of white smoke and burning sparks. I stop, distressed, and by the time I can see again, the train is already far away. It gives a sad wail goodbye. The girl's blond hair sparkles, all the way out there, and I cry because I have been left behind.

(The writer speaks)

In the thirties of the last century, the town of Munhango's small railway station was painted an intense, melancholy yellow, as if lit up on all sides by a perpetual sunset. Looking at it, no matter what time, travelers would experience a phantom nostalgia. They knew that they had never been there before, yet the sadness of the place made their souls ache. Almost all of them left the town with a feeling that they were abandoning some part of themselves. Years later, many would still smile – a rather sad smile – when they happened to recall their brief passage through Munhango: "Ah, that station in the Angolan interior, so beautiful! What was it called again?"

Encountering the words I have written above, an older reader might raise an eyebrow, irritated, before protesting that, no, no, in reality the station was painted in that dull pink, common to the majority of public buildings in the overseas territories. Sorry if I disappoint you: I don't give a damn about reality.

Loth Savimbi liked to sit at the station, in the cool shade of the small porch – "in the slow air," as he used to say, imitating the slightly unsteady Portuguese of one of his colleagues. He would sit there, reading the papers, after lunch, as the sun worked itself up against the iron of the tracks. It was there that old Francisca found him on the afternoon of August 3rd – "*Pai*," she called him, in her meek Umbundu. "Come quick, your wife Helena's had a son."

Even though he wasn't yet a stationmaster, a position to which he would be named in 1942, Loth Savimbi enjoyed a certain authority and respect from the colonizers and the children of the land alike, with the exception of Father Antero, a partly deaf, partly blind septuagenarian, who saw him as a fierce competitor in the ardent battle for the conquest of souls. Loth had studied at the Currie Instituto, in Dondi, founded in 1914 by Methodist ministers from the United States and Canada, becoming a pastor. He took religion extremely seriously. Wherever he went, he immediately commissioned a wattle-and-daub building to receive the faithful, and another, a smaller one, to house a school. The courtesy with which he treated everybody charmed whites and blacks, animists and Catholics alike, meaning it was natural, therefore, that the representatives of the Catholic Church would not look favorably upon him. The gossip of the priests explains the brevity of his stays in stations and waystations. Today it is still possible to trace this committed pastor's wanderings along the rosary of schools and churches he left behind: Cubal, Ambandi, Sapessi, Chipeio, Jilianga, Belmonte, Katele-Kalucinga, Salvador-Mussende, Gumba, Chivinga, Lonhoha, Vila

Alegre, Kalucinga, Vila Estrela, Bela Vista, Ekosa, Etumbuluko, Boa Esperança.

Loth's father, Sakaita Savimbi, had hated the Portuguese. The old man had fought on the side of Mutu-ya-Kevela in the Bailundo revolt of 1902, a dramatic event all but forgotten today but which at the time caused a great disturbance, both in the colony and up in the metropolis. If the testimony of the Angolan governor Francisco Cabral de Moncada, in *The Bailundo Campaign of 1902* (Lisbon, Livraria Ferin, 1903), is to be believed, everything started with Mutu-ya-Kevela's refusal to pay for a few small casks of spirits. The ovimbundo fighters began by attacking the homes and storehouses of the Portuguese traders based in the region. Many whites died. The survivors were led, hands and feet in chains, to Mutu-ya-Kevela, who joined them with the remaining slaves. I find it a curious irony of History that some of the last slaves in Angola were white.

A number of attacks were carried out on the Bailundo Fort and many hundreds died. On August 4th 1902, a Portuguese column, under the leadership of lieutenant Paes Brandão, succeeded in cornering Mutu-ya-Kevela. The "brave caudillo of black warfare" – as Francisco Cabral de Moncada called him, in recognition of his qualities as a military strategist – died with a bullet to the head.

Sakaita Savimbi kept half a dozen *canhangulo* single-shot rifles that had been used in the uprising. Sometimes he would overdo it on the drinking and return to the days of wrath. He would once again feel the blood beating in his neck. He could be seen shouting in the night, atop the cliffs, against the soldiers' camps. He heard the wails of the wounded, the crack of the sjambok marking the backs of Mutu-ya-Kevela's white slaves. Then he would load the old canhangulos and run through the fields firing into the air, cursing the war and the growing number of Portuguese who, bit by bit, were occupying his ancestors' lands. His hatred did not spare the priests, nor the protestant missionaries, most of them from the U.S.A., even though some of these were black and demonstrated a great interest in learning Umbundu.

(*Jonas Savimbi speaks*)

My grandfather, my grandfather Sakaita!

I see him approaching. Here he comes, tall, lanky, smacking the shadows away, and laughing and shouting in Umbundu, waving a rusty old canhangulo in the freshly washed morning air.

From my father I learned the art of dissembling, so essential in politics, and also in the command of men in a time of war. Loth also taught me to be ambitious. One day, I must have been seven or eight, I confessed my dream to him: I wanted to be an engine driver. All the boys in the world I grew up in had ambitions to drive locomotives. The railway line was creating worlds as it crossed the country. The drivers leaped out onto the station platform, sweating, coal-smeared, like heroes arriving from the future. The train ran our lives. Those men ran the trains. Loth, my father, didn't want to hear it: "You're going to be a doctor!"

At the time I thought it a startling folly.

As if he had said: "You're going to be a bird!"

Some days later, however, somebody asked me what I wanted to be when I grew up, and I didn't hesitate: "I'm going to be a doctor!"

My ambition, then, I owe to my father. The rebellion, to my grandfather Sakaita. I inherited my taste for speaking in proverbs from him, too.

"*Mbeu okulonda ko cisingi, omanu vokapako.*" A turtle can't climb trees on its own, somebody put it there.

(The writer speaks)

Goodness is transparent, it requires no explanation. Those whose souls are pure will tend, as we know, to provide weak characters. Pure souls, like pure water, don't taste of anything. They are an insipid matter. Wicked characters, on the other hand, are the delight of those actors who play them in the cinema or the theater. Evil, even of the most rudimentary kind, always seems much more complex and interesting than Good. The Devil fascinates us. As for the angels, well, they don't even have a sex.

The name Savimbi comes from "otchivimbi," which means "dead." The prefix "sa" means "father of." Hence, father of the dead. Jonas means "dove" in Hebrew.

At what point in his life was Jonas transformed into Savimbi?

I knew him.

I write these words and immediately notice their imprecision – I did not really know him. I only met him. What I'm doing now is trying to know him. The first time I shook his hand was on a distant afternoon, in Huambo airport. I remember myself, at this distance, a frighteningly thin young man, shy, with a birdlike profile and a very black, tempestuous head of hair. Jonas Malheiro Savimbi was at the peak of his forty-one years. I saw him arriving with an arm around Miguel N'Zau Puna, a pleasant man whose smile lit up everyone around him like a private sun. The Puna family takes pride in having descended from Mongovo Manuel Puna, dubbed Baron of Cabinda by D. Luís I of Portugal, and one of the signatories to the famous Treaty of Simulambuco. Miguel N'Zau Puna was, at the time, secretary-general of UNITA. He broke with the movement in 1992, shortly before the first elections, accusing his former comrade of a huge assortment of imaginative and terrible crimes. The two guerillas were in camo gear, with gleaming AK-47s slung over their shoulders. There were a lot of people. Everybody was clapping. Jonas Malheiro Savimbi came over to me and held out a hand. Each of the three movements had devised a different handshake as a hallmark. I got muddled up and greeted him with the MPLA handshake. He looked right at me, surprised, but said nothing. Then he walked on and forgot me.

We met again in 1995, at the 8th UNITA Congress in Bailundo. I was one of the few journalists credentialed to cover the event. Six years earlier, I'd put my name to a series of reports in the Lisbon weekly *África*, about two young UNITA dissidents, André Yamba Yamba and Armelindo Kanjungo, who had passed me witness statements and documents, including the diary of another militant, supposedly an agent of the movement's Political Police. One of the most appalling episodes of the civil war came to light as a consequence. The story was so implausible that when I first tried to publish it, in the Lisbon weekly *Expresso*, I was thrown out by the head of the international section, who today is working in Luanda for the *Jornal de Angola*: "This is propaganda from the Angolan government!" he shouted at me. "We don't accept Angolan government propaganda here!"

On September 7th, 1983, seven women and a boy were burned alive following accusations of witchcraft. The trial was held during a rally in Jamba – south-eastern Angola – where for many years

UNITA kept its most important base of operations. Jonas Savimbi presided over the rally, exhorting leaders and generals to light the flames.

In his first novel, *Patriots*, published in the U.K. in 1990, the writer José Sousa Jamba devoted a chapter to this event, a chapter that he himself decided, the following year, to excise from the Portuguese edition.

Jonas Savimbi was aware of my participation in the denunciation of the "witch-burning." In 1995, during the 8th UNITA Congress, he agreed to grant me an interview. He received me in a tent, surrounded by his generals, all of them with sullen expressions. He, however, never stopped smiling. His answers to my questions were shrewd and good-natured. I got the impression he wasn't telling me what he thought, but what he believed would please me. I remember, for example, asking him whether, looking back, he didn't regret the path he had taken. So much violence. Thousands dead. Mutilated. Orphans. He looked at me, his expression grave: "I am a soldier. Nobody hates war more than soldiers."

(*Jonas Savimbi speaks*)

It happened a long time ago. I woke up and saw one of my bodyguards perched in a tree. He opened his arms, flapped them about, and started to flutter from branch to branch. I got up. Dozens of soldiers, some of them naked, were pecking at the ground, and chirping and cawing to one another.

We later discovered that they'd eaten poisonous mushrooms. It was Vissolela, one of my wives – I've had many – who knew about mushrooms, and about herbs and roots. Without the things she knew, we'd have lost far more men during the Long March. Most of the soldiers died by nightfall. Five survived, but only one went back to being a person. The others stayed as birds. We used to see them, out in the fields, exercising their birdness noisily. Then one day I got annoyed and had them killed.

Birdie is the name of the one who went back to being a person. He stayed with me. Before the accident, he'd been called Hermenegildo Capelo Pena. Sometimes he suffers relapses. He sleeps in a squat, covered by a blanket. He has bird dreams. He says that he flies at night. He has something of a reputation for predicting inauspicious events. Yesterday, the day before yesterday, one of those nights, time's going in all directions at the moment, he asked to talk to me.

"They've betrayed us, old man. Our brothers, our own brothers, the ones born of our mamas, who grew up with us, who walked alongside us through the bush, who shared our hunger and suffering. They've sold us out. We're going to die."

I tried lifting his spirits:

"Yes," I said, "we're going to die. But we're going to die like men."

My words did not seem to console him.

"I'd rather die like a bird, old man. Oh, to die in flight! They say we go up to heaven when we die. I'd rather die in the heavens and after dying end up down on Earth."

(*The writer speaks*)

I published my first novel in 1989. In the years that followed, I've written another eight. I am often asked about my writing process, but I never know how to answer. It's my characters who write my books, I say, knowing that somebody is going to accuse me, right away, of rehashing clichés. I like clichés. Clichés are comforting, like a hug.

Sometimes our characters appear in our real lives, and by the time we've noticed, they're already embedded in the pages we're working on, chatting away, suffering, loving, leading the action. We understand at once that some of them do not belong to our universe. They are fantasy characters. They infiltrate reality through some artifice, or simply by mistake. The latter sort, the wayward ones, can't wait to get back to fiction. They look at a writer and see a crosser of borders. They seek us out so that we might lead them back over to the other side.

In other cases, they are so real that fiction rejects them. Most evolve. They arrive, adapt, prevail, and then, yes, then they do take over the action, subvert the screenplays, drag us through the mystery.

I was thinking about all this, sitting at one of the tables outside the Brasileira Café in Chiado, waiting for a friend, when I noticed a young woman, in the distance, coming up Rua Garrett. The sun was setting, clean and solemn, as she made her way through the crowd. She got distracted looking at the passersby, she stopped, dreamily, at the occasional shop window, she exchanged smiles with the street artists. Then she saw me, and walked purposefully in my direction.

"May I sit down?"

I got up. I offered her a chair. As I stood, the sky darkened and the wind began to blow. It was already raining by the time we had sat down again. The water was battering the broad blue awning, running, spilling onto the little paving stones, then rushing down the road in a violent commotion.

"What's happened to the summer?"

"Comes and goes," I replied. "Specially in winter."

We both laughed. She held out her right hand:

"Kassandra Sakaita Dachala. I've come a long way to meet you."

"I'm guessing we've both come from the Central Plateau. But I left longer ago. I'm older than you."

"Yes. Much older."

Her sincerity shocked me:

"Much? There's also no need to overdo it!"

Kassandra laughed:

"Very well, then, only a few years older. But actually I haven't come from the Central Plateau. I've never been on the Central Plateau. I was born in Johannesburg. I've lived in Paris, in Rome, in London, in Amsterdam. I'm currently residing in New York."

"You're Jonas Savimbi's daughter?"

"I am."

We fell silent. The rain disorganizing the silence. Kassandra had inherited her father's broad, expressive eyes. Her skin was soft and glowing. Her voice, too:

"I gather you're working on a new novel about my father."

"How do you know?"

"Because I read an interview where you talked about it."

"Oh yes, that's right."

"You said that writing about my father might perhaps help you to understand evil."

"Did I say that? I don't remember. But yes, I think so. We are born good. We become bad by an effort of the spirit. I think evil demands determination. Someone who is weak-spirited can't be very bad."

"Nonsense! Children are fierce! Animals are fierce."

217

I kept quiet. I hadn't been expecting her to challenge me. Kassandra took advantage of my silence. She raised her voice:

"We've already suffered a lot. Us, our family. How long are we going to have to keep on suffering?"

"I'm sorry. You, your family, you're also victims of the crimes Jonas Savimbi committed. But you cannot demand silence. We need discussion, a lot of it, we really do. It'd do us good to cry together. Only then will we be able to get past the pain."

"You didn't know him. My father was a generous man. He despised material things. He gave Angola everything he had. He let himself be killed for Angola."

"Was he a good father?"

"You're asking if he was a good father?!"

"Yes, was Jonas Savimbi a good father? Did he care about his children?"

"He had a lot of children . . ."

"Oh, no, please not that old speech, for the love of God . . ."

"Yes, the humble people of Angola. We, the Ovimbundo, the humble, despised people of Angola."

"Do you have any good memories of the time you spent with him? Were you together much?"

Kassandra threw me a terrible look. I was saved by the arrival of the friend I had arranged to meet. Sapalo Kapingala emerged before us from the rain, shaking off an elegant blue gabardine. He kissed Kassandra on both cheeks, clapped me twice very hard on the back and then, laughing a lot, took a chair:

"I see you've already made friends. Sorry I'm late. I had to swim here."

Sapalo studied Dramatic Arts in New York. After completing his course, he refused to come back to Luanda, where a secure but boring career in public television awaited him. Nor would he settle in Lisbon, the city that was home to some of the best Angolan actors. He went to Los Angeles. He struggled. In recent years he has managed to play half a dozen parts in low-budget productions. He also made three fiction shorts of his own. He had called me the day before. He happened to be in Lisbon and wanted to introduce me to a friend. I wanted to know why he'd hidden her identity from me. Kassandra smiled:

"I asked him not to tell you. I thought you'd refuse to speak to me."

"Why?"

"Because as you've already seen, I've only come here to annoy and confuse you. And you, sir, are an arrogant man, you think you own the truth."

219

"Choose another defect, just not that. I'm a writer, not a theologian or a judge. I don't look for the truth, a single truth, what I'm interested in are its different versions. Tell me yours."

(Kassandra Sakaita Dachala speaks)

My parents met in Johannesburg. I'm guessing that for Naiole, who was then very young, it would have been hard to resist the advances of a man like Savimbi. She admired him very much. She didn't love him, but she admired him very much. She got pregnant. I was born in 1980. A few weeks later, we moved to Paris. We lived a life with no troubles. My mother was on a scholarship from the movement to study Economics. In 1988 she was summoned to Jamba. She left me in Rome, in the care of an aunt, and never came back.

And what happened to her?

She fell in love – that's what I was told.

She fell in love in Paris with a diplomat of the movement called Daniel Epalanga. Naiole was always a real romantic. She would spend her days listening to Roberto Carlos. Savimbi learned of the affair. He had the lovers watched. He gathered evidence. Photographs. Copies of both their diaries. They were arrested the moment they arrived in Jamba. My mother was stripped and publicly flogged. That's what they say. They threw her into a pit and waited for her to die of hunger. Years later, Savimbi came through Lisbon and I went to see him. He embraced me, weeping: "My daughter! My daughter!"

He used to send me presents on my birthday. He would phone in the middle of the night. He took an interest in my studies. He knew how to make me laugh.

(Sapalo Kapingala speaks)

One of my grandfathers, a white man of Madeiran origin, a native of Lubango, was one of Mutu-ya-Kevela's slaves. I did actually get to meet him, when he was extremely elderly, but I barely remember him. A gentleman of sand, who spent the whole time sitting on the doorstep, laughing to himself and chatting with the birds. Joaquim started to go out with my grandmother in the period when he was a slave, and that was how our family came to be. My father fought in the war of liberation on the side of the Portuguese troops. He was an ensign. At the start of the civil war he joined the men of UNITA, also known as "The Black Rooster." He reached the rank of brigadier. He was there when they arrested and killed Daniel Epalanga. They took him to a little hut. The man showed no fear. He believed, per-haps, that he would get away with a simple reprimand. A few days in prison. At the most half a dozen months on weeding duty. An officer came to him in silence, holding an enormous rock, and threw it at the poor wretch's head. He fell. Then they dragged him outside and carried on beating him with the stone. They destroyed his face. Still he didn't die. They tied him to a tree. The giant ants climbed up from the ground and ate him. This man, Daniel Epalanga, had a wife and three small children. All four were buried alive.

(Jonas Savimbi speaks)

I'm falling, I'm almost asleep.

The birds have started singing again.

I make my way along a corridor, or a river, sometimes a corridor, other times a river. A dark light draws me through vast empty halls, floating islands, nights unleashing their winged insects against me. I see scales, wings, burned-out houses, and inside a startling amount of maggots. I hear the convulsed voice of the dead. I killed them.

Why did I kill them?

Because I could.

I remember playing football. Us, the kids from the Mission, against the whites from the regular school. We played better, much better, but we tried hard to lose so we could keep playing.

Then one day I said: "Today we're going to win!"

We won seven-two. The administrator's son put the ball under his arm: "You lot are never playing again."

I took the ball from him. The lad came toward me. I dodged, I pushed him and he fell. I kicked him right in the face. Blood came out. A powerful joy filled my chest, seeing him there on the ground, lips torn, trembling with fear and humiliation.

That night my father tore my clothes off, yelling. He lashed my back with a sjambok. I didn't care. What did bother me was my mother's silence. Her indifference.

So that is death: a river: and I'm going.

(*The writer speaks*)

Six months after my novel, *The Last Days of Jonas Savimbi*, was published, I received a letter from Kassandra Sakaita Dachala. She had moved to Luanda. She felt simultaneously repelled and amazed. She hated the noise, the chaotic traffic, the generators that made the verandas shudder, the yelling on the streets, the filth, the new buildings with neither personality nor elegance, advancing and, like a terrible disease, swallowing up the beautiful, austere colonial mansions. On the other hand she was fascinated by the city's life. She liked talking to people, rich and poor, because everybody seemed to her as though they'd just emerged from some fantasy. She was surprised not to find anybody judging her. They would look at her with curiosity as soon as they learned they were in the presence of one of Jonas Savimbi's daughters. They'd ask her a question or two and then forget the whole matter.

Kassandra had read the novel. Jonas Savimbi, the character, had not corresponded in almost any respect to the image she retained of her father. Here and there she recognized a gesture, a realistic piece of dialogue, which the next line, however, quickly dispelled. She supposed that I remained as ignorant about the origins of Evil as I had been when I began. "I don't know if it's a good novel or not," she concluded. "I know it's got nothing to do with my world. I feel like a foreigner when I read it, so distant from the characters, from the brutality, from all these people." I wrote to thank her for reading. I'm sure I'll meet her again one of these days, at the home of common friends, at a party, at some public reception. We won't speak of the book.

The Final Border

IT TOOK the border guard a while to grasp what was happening to him. He was sleeping. He was having an intense dream about something, or about several things at the same time – Charlize Theron's ass, chocolates, a sailing boat slipping across an emerald sea – when, all of a sudden, he found himself in a line of people waiting to cross a border. He presumed, with no particular alarm, that it was still the same dream but unfolding in some unforeseen way.

Death is like dreaming, but more so.

It seemed natural for the border guard that he should dream about borders. Lines of people. Passports. Stamps. A hunched figure in a guardhouse. He looked for his passport. He couldn't find it. This brought him a sudden distress.

"Well, it's only a dream," he muttered to his shoes.

Except he wasn't wearing any shoes. He was naked, him and the remaining rabble standing in the line. That was when he noticed that the guy in the guardhouse had a huge pair of white wings affixed to his back. Everything about him, indeed, was of an implausible whiteness. A natural angel, like the ones from those pious engravings his old aunt used to have.

"Ugh, what a shitty dream!" he murmured, then he felt sorry for having used a bad word when he saw the angel raise his transparent face and stare at him with a frown. The rabble ahead of him, likewise, threw him a hard, bitter stare. Old men and old women. Standing over there, one young guy who looked like a parking attendant who'd been run down by a truck.

"I should be the one in that guardhouse," he thought. "If that was me, none of these people would make it. I'd send them all back home. The junkie would be first to go."

Finally the angel gave him a slight nod and the guard stepped forward.

"Your sentiments, please," the angel asked, seemingly distracted, back bent under the weight of the wings.

"It's not *sen-ti*-ments, cretin! It's *do-cu*-ments."

The border guard was easily annoyed. It wasn't his fault, as he was constantly explaining to his bosses, each time some offended traveler complained, the problem was with his liver. As a child he'd contracted hepatitis twice and his liver had never recovered. Even these last few days it'd been really bad. An invincible tiredness, the whites of his eyes not as white as all that, like a grimy shirt, his skin similarly dull and yellow, his urine thick. Oh! And that irritability that so troubled him.

The angel shook his wings, a single sharp flick, which in him was surely a sign of an infinite displeasure.

"Excuse me?"

He said this in the splendorous language used by angels for communicating with heathens, but it felt as though they were words spoken in the language of Shakespeare by the haughtiest of British aristocrats: "I do beg your pardon?"

With more splendor, then, and even more panache. The border guard shuddered:

"I'm sorry, I didn't mean it. My liver, you know? I've got liver trouble."

"You used to have it," the impassive angel retorted. "You don't anymore."

"Wow, but it's *such* a shitty dream. And there's no need to frown, Mr. Guard Angel, and you too, damn rabble, your outrage doesn't scare me. This is just a shitty dream, yeah, a real shitty dream! I want to wake up and get out of here." He closed his eyes and pinched himself, with right thumb and index finger, on the left arm. When he opened his eyes, the angel was still in front of him, but he seemed more concrete now, more realistic than any border guard in any country had ever seemed to him before.

"Well, then. May I see your sentiments?"

The border guard felt a great urge to cry. He realized, with a violent clarity, that he was not going to be waking up again and he was overtaken by a deep nostalgia for long lines at the airport, for the smell of sweat, for the fear on those boorish faces, for the dry smack of stamps in passports.

"It's good, this system you got here," he said to the angel. He wasn't being ironic, nor was he flattering him. He was being quite sincere. "It's a good system, this business of all the passengers presenting themselves totally naked."

"Your sentiments, please . . ."

The border guard looked at the angel in silence. Slightly nervous. Sweating. Oh no, he wasn't hiding those feelings of his, he gave his word. Really he wasn't! He just had no idea where the hell he'd put them . . . The angel frowned at him again. He jotted something down in an impressive white-covered notebook.

"The gentlemen with no sentiments will have to wait in the room off to the side," he said. "The rest of you may go through."

The Best Bed in the World

THE MOMENT he opened his eyes, Melchior dreamed of a flock of herons taking flight from a salt marsh. In the dream, the salt marsh was an immense stretch of open country, all in a spotless white. He closed his eyes again. It was as if he had awoken into a larger dream. Those were the words he used, many years later, to describe to me what had occurred. He opened his eyes, saw himself surrounded once again by the unfailing whiteness, and only then did he remember what had happened to him the previous day.

He had gone hunting. He'd left very early in the morning, accompanied by Kim and Brazza, his two albino bloodhounds: "I returned as it was getting dark, looking for the truck, but I couldn't find it. At that moment I found myself lost."

Someone who finds himself lost, I thought, that's a nice oxymoron to define the human condition. But please excuse the digression. My grandmother did use to accuse me of suffering from philosophical follies: "Your good judgment is inflamed, girl. You're going to wind up an artist, like your grandpa, and frankly they're about as useful as raindrops on the sea." So Melchior went off in search of the truck and couldn't find it. He walked for two hours, fighting his way through elephant grass, taller than a man, with every step in the mud a struggle not to lose his boots, and after his boots his feet, until the night swallowed up all the colors and the scrubland burst out into a profusion of hoots and cries, clicks and howls.

"All I could see was the brightness of the dogs," he told me. "Thank God, their pelts gleamed in the nighttime. It was that gleam that saved me."

The dogs led him to a small hill. From the top, he spied the lights of a house, and the beaten-earth road connecting it to the world. He managed to reach the trail, and fifteen minutes later he was knocking at the door. The owner, a scrawny, somewhat cross-eyed man, held out his hand suspiciously, saying his name was Alípio, and apologizing for not being able to put him up. It was a small dwelling and he had six daughters. The gentleman would have to spend the night in the cotton storehouse. Melchior agreed. He didn't need much, he said, just a mat to stretch out on and a bucket of water to wash his face.

"I never could have imagined," Melchior told me, "what I would find there: the best bed in the world."

Three of Alípio's daughters brought him clean sheets, which they stretched out over an enormous pile of recently gathered cotton bolls. One of the girls, Natália, hung a mosquito net from a hook on one of the roof beams, while she warned Melchior to shake out his boots in the morning before putting them on, because very often the scorpions would hide inside them. The advice was unnecessary, yet the hunter thanked her for it tenderly, because it seemed to him almost a declaration of love.

That night, lying on the best bed in the world, Melchior slept badly. Falling asleep meant missing out on the moment. Lying there, his body floating on the cotton bolls, breathing in the fresh scent from the sheet, the memory of Natália's bright face came to him and it occurred to him that the citrus freshness was hers.

He awoke several times. Through a narrow open window over the storehouse door he watched the elation of the stars. He saw them, or thought he saw them, dancing in the night like drunken bees. In the uncertain half-light of the dawn, he saw an owl chasing a snake, and he understood then, with sudden clarity, that he was about to be reborn. That was what he told me, exactly that, those very words.

So Melchior awoke, early in the morning, dreaming of herons, he opened his eyes and closed them again, thinking he had fallen into a larger dream, and when he reopened them, as he was recalling everything that had happened the previous day, he saw Natália, dressed in white, with the two albino bloodhounds at her feet.

"All of us are born at least twice," he assured me, very seriously. For him, the second birth happened on the morning when he awoke in the best bed in the world and saw my grandmother beside the storehouse door, smiling at him.

Natália – a happy, practical woman, who went through her whole life without once being moved by a sunset – used to make fun of him:

"We drew lots, me and my sisters, to see which of us would wake the hunter up. It fell to me, and I went to do it, reluctantly. I've never liked hunters. I did not smile at him, that part's not true, I didn't even greet him. I held out an enamel cup, with hot coffee, and left."

They were married three months later, and went to live in Luanda, where my grandfather opened a photography studio. He was supposed to earn his living developing and enlarging photographs for his customers, taking pictures at weddings and baptisms, but Melchior spent more time busy with his own art, so that the store went bankrupt and it fell to Natália to struggle to support the family, making and selling sweets.

Melchior left me his photographs. They are, as they say, the portrait of an age. Unfortunately, there is no picture of that cotton store where my grandfather was born for the second time. Where, after all, my own story began.

The Fourth Angel

A FTER HE had created His first angel, God offered him a power-ful pair of wings. They were, He explained, a piece of equipment more of faith than of flight.

"Birds fly by conviction," He assured him.

The angel saw how birds flew, beating their wings and drawing in their legs, and he imitated them. After five months he had acquired a certain skill and was even able to do a few twirls, including a nose-dive followed by a double corkscrew loop. He wasn't exactly an eagle yet, but nor could he be mistaken for a chicken. In any case, he was flying.

"Now take them off," God said to him then, as He had been watching him, in silence, from a discreet distance, for all those days. "Take off your wings and fly."

The angel looked at Him incredulously. He protested:

"What the hell kind of nut-job do you think I am, eh, God? No way am I taking off shit! *Porra nenhuma*, you understand?"

233

God, who – as we know – is Brazilian, wasn't at all surprised that the angel should be swearing in Portuguese, not even with that strong Rio accent. After all, he'd picked up the language and accent from Him. But He understood that what he was lacking was the most essential thing, faith, along with slightly more polished manners, since, everything considered, he was still an angel after all, albeit one in an initialization stage, and with a rapid movement of annoyance, He uncreated him.

The second angel was, without a doubt, a more compliant, refined fellow. Extremely blond and fragile. An exceptionally angelic sort of angel. His hair was long, and he liked to keep it always clean and braided, in a most charming ponytail. He learned to fly more quickly than the first, using an original technique that put the birds to shame. However, when God told him to take off his wings and throw himself like that, totally naked, off a very high crag, he too refused.

"Oh, God! You must surely know, Lord, that I shan't be doing that. Oh, do forgive me, I'll do anything, anything, You understand? I'll do anything, but I'm not doing that, oh Lord, no."

He said all this in a tremulous, humble voice, with no trace of arrogance, so the Creator took pity on him and let him go. The angel painted his wings shocking pink and joined a flock of flamingos. They say you can still see him today, on certain fiery twilights, on some remote swamp in Africa, an angel flying, with singular elegance, among a cloud of flamingos. Flying and laughing. I've never seen him, but could be.

The third angel God made more practical, and bolder. He wore a curved mustache and he was a respectful being, of few words. He flew effortlessly, but also joylessly. He would come to rest on the branches of mango trees, or other trees that were equally tall and leafy, and he was quite capable of staying there, just sitting there, for whole afternoons, smoothing his impressive mustache, eating mangos and enjoying the cool shade and the birdsong. When God asked him to go up onto the highest crag and take off his wings and jump, he didn't answer Him. He said nothing. He flew up to the crag, took off his wings, and jumped. It became clear, in that one tragic moment, that what he possessed abundantly in discipline he lacked in faith. Or rather, as God tried to explain to him as he fell, precipitously, against the ferocious cutting rocks, all the way down at the bottom, the problem was that he had put all his faith in the equipment instead of putting it in the purpose. The impact was devastating.

The Lord God was sorrowful at this latest debacle. It took him a long time to recover. At last, he tried again. The angel that came out, on his fourth attempt, was happy, perhaps even a bit of simpleton, who liked singing and dancing most of all, arts that, in fact, he had himself invented. Flying didn't seem to be something for which he had any particular aptitude. However, when God suggested that he take off his wings and try flying without them, using the effort of faith, he merely asked, stunned:

"Is that really possible?"

Then he shed his wings, looked down into the deep abyss, shut his eyes, and imagined that within his body there were other wings unfurling and beating. It was with these wings, a little twistily, a little tipsily, that he rose up into the sky.

God rejoiced. After this angel He made many others, legions and legions, but few of them, very few, were capable of imitating number four. It is said that this wingless angel moves among us, like a kind of secret agent. An observer on the battlefield. An anonymous witness.

Angel number two is probably happier.

Matulai, the South Wind

ABACAR ABUBACAR knows all the winds. He knows them by name, by origin, and by temperament. He knows them better than he knows his own children, whom, as it happens, he hasn't seen in many years. He was born on a dhow, and since then has spent more time living on the sea than on terra firma. He doesn't like the expression "terra firma." He doesn't feel safe on land. Only the sea seems firm to him.

"How many people do you know who have been shot dead while at sea? Or got run over while fishing?"

When night falls, he drops anchor at a safe distance from the land, at least a hundred meters away, and only then does he stretch out on the coarse wood, and sleep.

His sleep is deep and dreamless. When he wakes, he asks the fish about the winds. Since the fish are wise they tell him things he has always known. Abubacar enjoys the discreet wisdom of the fish.

One morning he wakes up and sees no fish. No birds. The silence, like a blanket, covers the clear calm of the waters. He wonders where the fish might be. Where the winds have gone. He wonders if the world still exists.

Or, he thinks, perhaps he has died? Maybe this is what death is: a sea with no fish.

For the first time, he is afraid of the sea.

He sits and waits. In this motionless time, upon the lifeless liquid, he hears a voice that seems to come from everywhere:

"Who's there?" asks the voice.

Abubacar gives a start. The voice seems familiar.

"Who's there?" he asks in turn.

"I asked first," the voice objects.

"Abacar," says Abacar. "Abacar Abubacar."

"Abacar, the fisherman?"

"Yes . . ."

"The friend of the winds?"

Abacar senses a slightly ironic tone to the voice. He can't tell if it is mockery or praise.

"Well, nobody knows *all* the winds," he murmurs, a little irritated. "I only know our own. I don't know a thing about foreign winds."

"And what are you doing here?"

"What am I doing here? I live here! This is my sea."

"Not this sea, Abacar. Not this one. Not yet."

Abacar stands up, very nervous. He spreads his eyes across that tranquil emerald mirror. It's then that anguish strikes his heart like an enemy arrow. No, this is not the sea where he was born and where he has lived his whole life. It's the same color and has the same wonder. There is the narrow island and, beyond it, the leisurely outline of the continent. Yet it lacks the whisper of the winds, the dense murmur of the fish crossing the currents, the powerful smell of salt and life that, every morning, brings him more energy than a cup of coffee.

The island is a time capsule. Nothing of the present can reach us here. From time to time tourists show up. We don't ask them from where they've come, but from when. Naturally they come, all of them, from some moment in the future. However, when they dock here, they no longer remember. Journeys through time provoke an irreversible kind of amnesia.

Abacar is well-acquainted with that illness. He has transported such wayward tourists often. They look in wonder at the rocks raised up at the surface of the waters, like the lightest pieces of filigree, delicate roses of stone, and they ask:

"Is this possible?!"

Abacar knows it isn't a question of possibility, but of patience. Those people come from an impatient time. They don't understand the work of the centuries.

"Where am I?" he asks at last.

The air seems to roar with laughter around him. The boat rocks slightly. In that unfamiliar water, an inanimate copy of his own sea, Abacar feels like an avocado tree retreating completely back into the inside of the avocado. He understands with horror, and relief, that the voice surrounding him is his own.

He sits on the prow, with his feet brushing the water, and shuts his eyes. He smiles when he hears the wind. He knows it well: it is Matulai, the good south wind, the one that combs the waves, untangles the knots in thoughts, and puts women in better humor. He smiles, before he has even opened his eyes, because he knows he's back home. Three hours and he'll be mooring on the jetty. Aisha will appear with a bowl of seaweed matapa and new logs, wide-hipped and ample-bosomed, her great laughter unsubdued. At night his sleep would be deep and dreamless. And in the morning he would talk to the fishes.

archipelago books
is a not-for-profit literary press devoted to
promoting cross-cultural exchange through innovative
classic and contemporary international literature
www.archipelagobooks.org